T0117053

Black Sails at Midnight

A. J. Glazer

authorHOUSE®

AuthorHouse™ UK Ltd.
500 Avebury Boulevard
Central Milton Keynes, MK9 2BE
www.authorhouse.co.uk
Phone: 08001974150

First published by AuthorHouse 4/5/2011

ISBN: 978-1-4567-7673-2 (sc)

Chapter One
A Pirate's Tale

Captain Will Morgan was one of the most infamous Pirates the world has ever known. It all began in the town of Portsmouth. He was born William James Morgan on the 3rd May 1770; he was an only son. His Mother was very caring and loved her son beyond measure and the feeling was mutual; his Father on the other hand was a violent drunk, who often beat his wife.

When William was 12 years of age, his Father sent him to the workhouse to earn him some money, where he would work 15 hours a day for pennies and when he got home his Father would take his money off him to buy his drink. This went on for years. With no way of having a proper education or childhood, what chance did he have in life.

As the years went by William got stronger, in body and mind. When he was 16, he got home from the workhouse late one day. His Father was fuming and he set upon William.

When his Mother stepped in to protect him, his Father turned around and lashed out at her, she fell back and with a mighty thud hit her head on the mantelpiece above the fireplace; she then collapsed to the floor with a pool of blood under where her head lay.

William rushed over to her and knelt down beside her trying to revive her, but it was to no avail; she was dead. He cradled her lifeless body in his arms, sobbing.

"Leave her be" ordered his Father and without an iota of remorse, added "she deserved it."

William's face then turned from a look of sorrow to a look of anger. He turned to his Father and in a fit of temper he picked up a poker from the fireplace and lashed out at his Father, striking him in his forehead with all his might and his Father fell like a sack of potatoes onto the floor.

This commotion was heard outside and a passer-by contacted the authorities, the next minute two soldiers were knocking at the door. One of them looked through the window and was looking eye to eye at William, who was still holding the bloody poker. William looked down at the poker he had in his hand and not knowing what to do, he dropped the poker, turned and ran out the back door with the soldiers in pursuit.

He ran as fast as his legs could carry him, through alleys to try to evade his pursuers, looking over his shoulder every now and then to make sure he had lost them. He knew that if they caught him he would get the blame for both of their deaths, so he has to get as far away as possible. He was too young to face the gallows.

He headed for the docks; they were very busy, so he could hide there. He was now a wanted man. There was a galleon anchored in the docks, called the 'Audacious', so he saw a way to get out of the country. He didn't know or care where it was going.

He walked up to it and waited, when he was sure nobody was looking, he sneaked aboard and found a place to hide below decks until they set sail. When he was sure they were out of reach of land, he emerged on deck.

He tried to blend in with the crewmen but was spotted by the Captain, who did not recognise the face.

"You boy!" Shouted the Captain. "Come here."

William hesitantly approached the Captain.

"You're a stranger here, I do not recognise you. You are not one of my crew, what might you be called?" Asked the Captain.

"William, Sir." He replied.

"William what?" Said the Captain.

"William Morgan, Sir." Replied William.

"Well William Morgan Sir. First thing is don't call me Sir, my name is Captain John Kidd; Captain to you. How did you get on board?" Asked the Captain.

"I walked on when nobody was looking." Replied William.

"I admire your nerve, but give me one reason why I shouldn't put you back ashore." Said Captain Kidd.

"I cannot go back" said William "I have nothing to go back to, both my Parents are dead; Can I stay here? I will work for my passage, I am a good worker."

Captain Kidd agreed to let him stay and took him under his wing; he was to teach him how to fight to be stronger.

The next day Captain Kidd went up to William's bunk and shook him to wake him up in the early hours. William fell out of his bunk and with a dull thud hit the floor.

"Are you awake?" Asked Captain Kidd, sarcastically.

"Aye Captain." Replied William.

"Good" said the Captain "then we will go on deck and practise your swordplay."

They went up on deck; Captain Kidd was holding two swords. He held them up in the air and tossed one of them to William, who only just caught it by the hilt.

"Good; at least you can catch" said the Captain "now let's see if you can use it properly."

They crossed swords, then Captain Kidd told William to attack him and try to kill him. They both stepped back until they were the right distance from each other, then

William lunged at the Captain, who blocked the lunge and swept William's sword out of his hand and onto the deck.

"You are not holding it tight enough" said the Captain, sternly "tighten your grip and have some movement in your wrist."

They began again and William was improving slowly. They were clattering their swords together. William pushing the Captain back, then the Captain pushing William back, until they got into a deadlock with their swords locked together and Captain Kidd pulled a dagger out of a sheath and held it against William's gut.

"That's cheating!" Said William.

"The first rule in swordplay" said Captain Kidd "expect the unexpected. This ends our first lesson. You did well for a beginner. I think it will not be long before you are ready. We will have another lesson tomorrow."

They practised every morning and William was improving with every lesson. He will soon be an expert in this field of warfare.

Two weeks into their voyage, Captain Kidd and William were sitting in the Captain's quarters, when a voice was heard. "SHIP AHOY!"

Captain Kidd told William to stay below and then went on deck. "Pass me the spyglass." He said to the First Mate. Through the spyglass he saw a British Man-of-War. It was heading straight for them.

"Hoist up the Union Jack, when we get them broadside we will hoist up our colours and attack." Ordered Captain Kidd.

When they got broadside of them, they hoisted up their colours, it was the Jolly Roger. *They were Pirates*. William heard a lot of commotion on deck, so he put his head up to see what was going on and he saw the Jolly Roger hoisted on the mast and a lump came to his throat. What has he done? He then knew there was no going back. He had inadvertently stowed away aboard a Pirate ship. His adventure begins.

He went back down into the Captain's quarters; He was not yet ready to fight. There was much noise outside, the sound of cannon fire, gunfire and the clatter of swords. William sat on a bench, shaking, not knowing what was going to become of him. After what seemed an eternity, there was silence and William did not know what to expect; who was going to walk through the door?

The door opened and in walked Captain Kidd, there was blood on his arm.

"You've been wounded, Captain." Said William, worriedly.

"It's just a flesh wound" replied the Captain "I will get it patched up in no time. So now you know who we are, are you disappointed?"

"No." Replied William, and he then told Captain Kidd the real reason he sneaked on board, because there was no way he would turn him in.

Captain Kidd took William on deck, where his men had hauled the bounty. He could not believe his eyes; there were two large chests of jewels and gold coins. It seemed that the British Man-of War was transporting it to England in payment for arms to fight a revolution in Mexico.

"There is more money than I could dream of here!" Said William, flabbergasted.

"This is what we do" said Captain Kidd "if you want to join us, you could have a share too. I will teach you all I know. You have spirit and you will make a good Pirate."

"I would like that." Said William.

Captain Kidd put his arm around William's shoulder and led him down to the Captain's quarters. He took out a bottle of rum and two glasses, then he half filled the glasses with the rum and handed one of them to William.

"Here William" he said "let us drink to our new friendship."

William took one slug of the rum and nearly choked on it. He had never had any alcohol before. Captain Kidd patted his back. "That will put hairs on your chest, lad." He said. Captain Kidd was to treat William like the son he never had.

One year had passed, Captain Kidd had taught William all he could about fighting, including the dirty tricks; he was becoming quite the expert.

Back in England; a Captain James Bart was preparing to set sail. His orders were to pursue and capture Captain John Kidd and his band of cut-throats and bring them to justice. Failing that, he is to bring Captain Kidd's body back.

Captain Bart was a big man with short black hair and a hard face. He was a veteran of the Navy; a very experienced mariner and a very determined man. He will not let anything stand in his way; but he can sometimes be a bit foolhardy, which may be his downfall.

He was given the HMS. Indestructible; an 'A' class forty gun galleon.

They set sail from the Naval base at Portsmouth, heading across the Atlantic. Captain Bart stood at the bow looking ahead of them, standing straight up with his large stomach protruding out and his hands behind his back and a tricorn hat perched on his head.

They sailed for days without sighting anything, through calm waters and stormy waters; until on the seventh day, the lookout called down from the crow's nest. "Ship ahoy!"

Captain Bart took out his spyglass, placed it to his right eye and scanned the horizon. "There she is!" He shouted.

"All hands on deck. Load the guns. Hard to port and full sail ahead" then added "Raise the white flag."

His First Mate looked at him in a disturbing manner, wondering what he was up to, but gave the order anyway because he trusted his Captain.

As they neared the Audacious; Captain Kidd had spotted them and he saw the white flag raised.

"Ship ahoy!" He cried.

William rushed up to the poop deck to be with his Captain. "What's wrong?" He asked.

"There is a ship approaching fast" said Captain Kidd "it is flying a white flag. It may be a trap; order the gunners to prepare the guns. We will see what they have to say first."

"Load the guns and prepare to fire on the Captain's order!" William shouted.

The Indestructible came closer and closer until they were broadside of the Audacious, then Captain Bart shouted across to the Audacious. "I would like to speak to a Captain John Kidd."

Captain Kidd replied. "That is me."

"I am here to demand your unconditional surrender." Said Captain Bart.

Captain Kidd started to laugh out loud and the rest of the crew joined in, making a mockery of Captain Bart. "You have a sense of humour!" Shouted Captain Kidd.

"Do not mock me!" screamed Captain Bart "I am Captain James Bart of His Majesty's Navy and I demand your surrender!"

"What will happen if we do not wish to surrender to you on this day?" Enquired Captain Kidd.

"Then we will blow you and your crew out of the water" replied Captain Bart "but before we do, there is one more thing." He added; then turned to the crew of the Audacious and said "I have the authority to grant a pardon to anyone who turns Captain Kidd over to me. What say you?"

Captain Kidd turned to his crew and said. "Do you want to give him your answer?"

The lead gunner said. "Aye aye Captain" then ordered "FIRE!"

All the guns on the Audacious fired simultaneously, ripping gaping holes in the Indestructible and taking down the mast which held the white flag. The crew scattered; some of them leaping into the sea.

"You can't attack a ship bearing a white flag!" Shouted Captain Bart, then shouted at his crew who had dispersed "come back you cowards and fight!"

"We are Pirates!" Said Captain Kidd "the white flag means nothing to us."

The few crew that remained on the Indestructible fired back on the Audacious, but with not much effect because most of their guns were put out of action. The Indestructible then began to sink, aft first. Captain Bart still stood on the poop deck, upright with his hands behind his back. He was going down with his ship.

Moments later, the Indestructible disappeared into the deep blue ocean and all that was left of Captain Bart was his hat, which floated to the top of the water.

Captain Kidd turned to William and said. "What was the name of that ship?"

William replied. "I think it was the Indestructible."

"It didn't live up to its name." Said Captain Kidd, then the crew all laughed and began to sing "*yo ho he ho*" as they carried on their way, picking up the survivors of the Indestructible as they went.

Captain Kidd assembled the survivors on the main deck and said to them. "We are not savages. We will put you ashore on an island with some supplies, where you can wait for a ship to pass by and pick you up."

One of survivors shouted up to the Captain. "Can we join you, we are good seamen and very loyal."

Captain Kidd replied back "I saw how loyal you are. You all leapt into the sea at the first sign of trouble; leaving your Captain all alone on his ship."

The man, who seemed to be the spokesman for the survivors said "Captain Bart was an idiot. He thought he was immortal."

"How do I know I can trust you?" Said Captain Kidd.

"You can keep a watch on us and try us out" replied the man "what have you got to lose. There are not enough of us to cause you a problem."

"Very well" said Captain Kidd "we can use a few more men, but we will be watching you and if you cross us then there will be no mercy. You will wish we had put you ashore on an island full of cannibals."

They docked in a place called Tortuga, an island in the Caribbean, a haunt for many ruthless Pirates. They needed supplies.

Captain Kidd sent some of his men to get the supplies whilst he and William went to the local tavern for some refreshments.

Whilst sitting in the tavern, Captain Kidd overheard someone talking about a cargo of gold so valuable that the Governor himself will be accompanying it, being transported from England to the new lands in the 'Endeavour', a fully armed ship; it was to be heavily guarded.

It would certainly be a challenge, but the rewards will be great. This man had worked in the gold refinery in London and had got his hands on a map of the route they were going to take.

The man had a big mouth; he was either drunk or he wanted to try to trick someone into trying to attack the ship and steal the treasures, which would be a trap; but they had to decide if it was worth the risk.

Captain Kidd decided that it was and he had an idea to distract this man, so he walked over and sat beside him; then pushed a jug of ale in front of him and began talking to him, asking about this ship he was spouting on about, then William slid his hand into the man's pocket and slowly extracted the map from his pockets with not much trouble. It was maybe a bit too easy.

When they got all the supplies they required, they went back to their ship and set sail eastwards towards England to meet the Endeavour, studying the map they had stolen so that they did not miss their prey.

After three days at sea, they spotted something on the horizon, it was a ship. Captain Kidd looked through the spyglass and saw that it was a British ship. "That must be the one" he said "are you ready for a bit of action William to put into practice everything I taught you?"

"Aye aye, Captain." Replied William.

They set a course to intercept the ship. As they got closer, Captain Kidd looked through the spyglass. It was indeed the Endeavour.

"I can't see anyone on board" he said "something is wrong, we'll get closer, but everyone must be on their guard; make sure the guns are loaded and ready to fire."

They pulled up alongside the ship, they still could not see anyone. "This looks like a trap" said the Captain, then told the lead gunner "I will take some men and board the ship, any sign of trouble, fire on them."

The Captain took William and a handful of men and boarded the ship, when on board it seemed empty, then all of a sudden, out of nowhere, came men with swords, knives and guns blazing. The cannons fired on the Audacious, bringing down its centre mast. The Audacious fired back drilling holes in the hull and hitting some of the Endeavour's cannons and crew, putting them out of action.

Back on deck, Captain Kidd and his men had their hands full. William was so confident now, that he was taking on three at the time, which he had to since they were heavily outnumbered. Captain Kidd has taught him well.

After a long battle, there were bodies strewn around the deck. There was no sign of the Governor, so Captain Kidd and William went down to the cargo hold to find the treasure, but there was none.

"It looks like we have been set up." Said William.

"It looks that way." Replied Captain Kidd.

They heard a cry from the deck. "Captain, there's a ship approaching fast. It looks like a British Man-of-War." Captain Kidd and William rushed up the steps and onto the deck.

"Pass me the spyglass." Captain Kidd said to his man. He put it up to his eye "It is" he said "and it's after us. Everyone back to the Audacious."

They swung over to the Audacious, put the sails up, although one of their masts was down. They did not have enough sail to outrun the Man-of-War, which started firing upon her, missing by a whisker with every shot and throwing water all over the deck.

"Hard to port" ordered Captain Kidd "full sail ahead."

There was an island in front of them with a sheltered bay; they headed for it and hid behind a jagged cliff, in wait to ambush the Man-of-War.

"Turn to starboard" Captain Kidd ordered "load the guns and be prepared to fire. When the Man-of-War comes into view let her have everything we have got. If we catch her by surprise we may just defeat her."

They waited patiently because they knew that the British Man-of-War will eventually find them and their firepower is too great for them, but if they catch them by surprise they might just defeat them.

They were waiting and waiting patiently until the bow of a ship came into view past the cliff; the unsuspecting occupants slowly sailing into a trap.

"Wait until you see all of the ship" Captain Kidd ordered the gunners "then let them have it with everything we have got, on my word."

The Man-of-War slowly showed a bit more of herself with every second, unaware of what was waiting for her in the bay; until it was almost completely visible to the Pirate ship. The lookout on the British Man-of-War then spotted them, but before he could raise the alarm a shout came from the Audacious.

"FIRE!" Ordered Captain Kidd.

All the guns blazed at the same time, the air was thick with smoke. After the first salvo, Captain Kidd ordered them to reload then fire at will, which they did and yet more smoke filled the air until nobody could see anything.

When the smoke cleared, the damage became clear; the British Man-of-War was in pieces and on its way down to the bottom of the sea with its crew; it never stood a chance.

There were cheers of victory aboard the Audacious and they began to sing as they set sail again. "*Fifteen men on a dead man's chest, Yo ho ho and a bottle of rum. Drink and the devil had done for the rest, Yo ho ho and a bottle of rum.*"

They sailed towards the Caribbean a happy lot and docked in Jamaica to carry out repairs on their mast and to relax. They all invaded the tavern for some merriment and jugs of ale and grog.

Captain Kidd and William entered the tavern and walked up to the bar counter, then looked around the room, eyeing up all the ugly, ruthless faces until one face stood out, a man sitting in the corner with his head tilted down. It was the man who had set them up.

Captain Kidd took a piece of paper out of his pocket and drew something on it and folded it in half; then he called one of the serving girls over, handed the paper to her and told her to take it to the man.

She walked over to the man's table, placed the paper on it, slid it in front of him and said, pointing "this is from that man over there."

He unfolded the paper and what he saw on it gave him such a look of terror on his face. It was the black spot, a death sentence.

He raised his head to see who had given him this death sentence and saw Captain Kidd and William Morgan standing at the bar, staring at him, then his face went as white as a sheet as if he had seen a ghost; or two in this case.

The man slowly rose from his seat and headed towards the door and out onto the street; once outside, he quickly looked left then right for somewhere to run and hide. Straight ahead of him was a street with a lot of alleyways, so he headed for them to try to evade his pursuers.

Captain Kidd and William followed him outside and watched as he disappeared down an alley and still they followed.

They eventually caught up with him. William grabbed his arm and swung him against a wall and pinned him down. The man was shaking in his boots, wondering what was going to happen to him; ruing the day he decided to cross Captain Kidd.

"Who are you working for?" Demanded Captain Kidd. "Who told you to set us up?"

"It was Admiral Roswell" replied the man, with a tremble in his voice "he said I would be for the gallows if I didn't. I didn't want to, but I didn't want to die either; I had no choice, you have to believe me. I am begging you to spare my life."

"You have violated the Pirates code." Said Captain Kidd, then took out a dagger from a sheath on his belt and plunged it into the gut of the man, who then slid down the wall and rested on the ground with his back slumped against the wall. Captain Kidd withdrew his weapon, wiped the blade clean on the traitor's shirt then placed it back in its sheath. "The penalty for that is death." He said, looking down at the man.

"He was a snivelling treacherous coward. He won't be betraying any more Pirates now" Captain Kidd said to William "let us get back to the revelry at the tavern."

"Aye." Replied William.

They went back to the tavern, leaving the traitor's body where it lay. After a few jugs of ale, Captain Kidd started to sing. "*What shall we do with the drunken sailor, what shall we do with the drunken sailor, what shall we do with the drunken sailor, early in the morning.*" and the rest of the Pirates joined in "*heave ho and up she rises, heave ho and up she rises, heave ho and up she rises, early in the morning.*"

Within minutes the inn was filled with a raucous noise of dozens of drunken Pirates trying to sing.

A good time was had by all and they would all be suffering the next day on board ship.

Meanwhile the news got back to Admiral John Roswell, a stout man with a hard face and a bushy beard. His assistant Charles Broughton brought him the news.

"Damn!" Shouted the Admiral, slamming his fists on the desk "I want these Pirates, dead or alive." Then turned to Charles and said, sternly. "Find Captain Meriwether and bring him to me."

Captain Meriwether shouldn't be too hard to find, he just had to look around the Inns in the area.

He had become a drunkard since he was thrown out of the Navy for something he didn't do. The Navy was all he knew and it destroyed his life. He was a tall man with long black hair and brown eyes; he had a scar above his right eye.

Charles started his search for the Captain; he didn't know him, but he had a good description of him to recognise him. He thought to himself what would the Admiral want with a drunken lout, but he must be something special for the Admiral to ask for him personally.

After hours of searching the Inns, he finally reached the Mucky Duck Tavern in the East End. He entered the Tavern, looked around and saw one man sitting on his own in the corner, looking sorry for himself. He had a bottle of rum and a glass that was half full on his table in front of him; Charles Broughton recognised him from the description; he walked over and sat down opposite him at his table.

"Captain Meriwether?" Charles asked "George Meriwether?"

"Mister Meriwether" the Captain replied, slurring his words "I am no longer in His Majesty's Navy. Who wants to know anyway?"

"I am Charles Broughton. Admiral Roswell sent me to find you" said Charles "he has an assignment for you."

"Roswell?" Said George, a little surprised to hear that name again. "How is the old man?"

"He is well" replied Charles "but he has a major problem."

"What problem?" Asked George.

"With Pirates" said Charles "they are the Bain of his life, that's why he wants you."

"Why me, isn't there anyone else in his precious Navy that can do the job?" Said George.

"He has sent many ships after them but they never returned." Said Charles.

Meriwether sat silent for a few moments, picked up his glass, tipped it down his throat and half filled it again, then he looked up at Charles and gave him his answer.

"Very well, I will see him" said George "for old time's sake. I owe him that, he spoke in my defence at my court martial; tell him I will see him tomorrow at noon. Now leave me alone, I have better things to do, like get drunk."

Charles stood up and turned towards the door of the Tavern and on his way out he shook his head and thought to himself why does Admiral Roswell want this drunk. Surely he would be a liability, but who is he to question the Admiral's authority.

After Charles Broughton left, George clenched a fist around the bottle of rum, picked it up, looked at it then put it back on the table and pushed it to the other side of the table and went up to his room to go to bed. He has to be quite sober and with a clear head when he meets the Admiral so that he doesn't say or do anything he may regret.

He was staying at the Tavern because it belonged to a friend of his who lets him stay rent free, which is just as well because he hasn't got much money left.

The next day, Captain Meriwether went to see Admiral Roswell, who was looking a bit agitated, pacing up and down his office.

"Welcome George, thank you for agreeing to see me" said Admiral Roswell "it has been a long time. I called for you because I have a problem. I would like you to go after Pirates, I have pulled some strings in the Admiralty and they have agreed to reinstate you and give you a small fleet to command. If you are successful, you will keep your rank and your job. I will understand if you tell me to go to hell after all that happened, but I am asking you as a friend and it will give you back your self respect."

"This must be very important to the Admiralty, but give me one reason why I should accept this commission" said Captain Meriwether "after what they did to me."

"The Pirate in question is an old friend of yours. It's Captain Kidd" said the Admiral "anyway, what have you got now? Spending all your time in Inns, getting drunk, you have no friends; you have nothing to lose and if you are successful, you will be given your commission and your self respect back."

"Captain Kidd?" Said George, surprised to hear his name. "I have been after him for years; I would like to see him in hell."

George thought for a while, then said "Ok, I'll do it, when do I start?"

"Tomorrow" said Admiral Roswell "you can join your fleet at Portsmouth; Captain Kidd was last seen in the Caribbean, so you can start your search there, Charles will go with you as First Mate."

Captain George Meriwether and his First Mate, Charles Broughton travelled down to Portsmouth the next morning to join the fleet. They reached the docks, found the Harbourmaster and handed over the papers of authorisation. The Harbourmaster led them to their ship, the HMS. Invincible, a heavily armed Frigate, and his fleet which included four other ships, HMS. Diligence, HMS. Gallant, HMS. Illustrious and HMS. Victory, all Frigates.

Captain Meriwether and Charles met the Captains of the other ships in the fleet and informed them of their orders before they set on their quest, then they boarded the ship and met their crew and prepared to set sail.

"Anchors aweigh, set a course for the Caribbean." Captain Meriwether ordered. "Full sail ahead."

Chapter Two

On Devil's Ground

Back on the Audacious, everybody was the worse for wear after the jollities. William went down below for a rest to sleep it off, there was one of the men looking over something.

"What have you got there?" Asked William.

"Nothing." The man said, hiding it behind his back.

"You have something there, let me see it." Demanded William.

The man handed it over, reluctantly.

"This is a map" said William "it looks like a treasure map. Where did you get it?"

"I found it on one of the men on the Endeavour." He said.

"Why didn't you hand it in to the Captain?" Asked William.

"I didn't think it was important." Said the man.

"What's your name?" Asked William.

"Jim Parker." The man said.

"Well Jim Parker" said William "I will have to show this to Captain Kidd. He will not be very happy you tried to hide this from him." The sleep will have to wait.

William went back up on deck with the map to show the Captain, who scanned over it, then stood back in amazement, not believing what he is seeing in front of him.

"It can't be!" He said, excitedly.

"What is it?" Asked William.

"It's a map of the treasures of the Conquistadors" said the Captain "it's been missing for a hundred years. It is said that there is more gold and jewels than you can imagine and it looks like it's not far from here; where did you get this map?"

"This man had it" William said, pointing to Jim Parker "he said he found it on one of the men on the Endeavour."

Captain Kidd looked at Jim Parker with dagger eyes and said abruptly "Did you try to hide this from me?"

"No, Captain" replied Mr. Parker, nervously "I was going to bring it to you."

"Why did you not bring this to me straight away?" Asked Captain Kidd.

"I didn't know what it was." Replied Jim Parker.

"I hope you are not lying to me. You know the consequences if you are" said Captain Kidd "I will be keeping an eye on you."

William pointed to a spot on the map. "What are these?" He said.

"They look like mountains" said Captain Kidd "but there aren't any in this area."

William looked at the map again. "What's this triangle?" He said, spotting a faint outline of a triangle on the map.

Captain Kidd had a closer look. "God help us!" He shouted. "That's the Devil's Triangle and the treasure is right in the middle of it."

"What's the Devil's triangle?" William asked.

"It is said that any ship that enters the Devil's Triangle is never seen again" said Captain Kidd "there is evil like you have never seen before."

"Do you believe it?" Said William.

"I don't know if it is true" said Captain Kidd "but if we are to go after the treasure I will have to put it to the vote, anyone that does not want to go will be put ashore in Jamaica. If we go after the treasure, there is a real possibility that many of us will not return or perhaps none of us will."

Captain Kidd called all of his men on deck and told them everything then asked for a show of hands. It seemed like they were all loyal to their Captain because every single one of his men voted to go; or maybe it was just greed.

The next day, Captain Kidd let his crew go ashore to enjoy themselves before they begin their perilous journey, from where many may not return. He and William also went ashore, they went to have an ale in the Dirty Dick inn. They sat at a table and Captain Kidd spotted a man at another table watching them, a man with a bushy black beard, he was having a drink with some of his men.

"Do you see that man over there?" Said Captain Kidd, pointing with his eyes so that he didn't attract attention. "That's Edward Teach, otherwise known as Blackbeard, you should keep as far away from him as possible."

"I've heard about him, I heard he would kill his own Mother for a single gold piece." Said William.

"You heard right" replied Captain Kidd "he is pure evil."

While they were talking about Captain Blackbeard, he was keeping his beady eyes on them. What is this interest he has in Captain Kidd. Perhaps it is that he has heard about the map, but from whom.

They decided to join their ship and stay anchored for the night. The next morning, they repaired the mast, then Captain Kidd took some men to replenish their supplies, leaving William in charge while he was gone. When they got back, the Captain gave the order to weigh anchor and set sail.

They made their way out of the bay and headed towards the Devil's Triangle. In the distance behind them, five figures appeared on the horizon. It was Captain Meriwether and his fleet. The lookout on the Invincible had spotted the Audacious.

"Ship ahoy!" He shouted.

Captain Meriwether put his spyglass to his eye. "That's them, full sail ahead." He ordered, then signalled to the other ships in the fleet.

The lookout on the Audacious spotted the fleet approaching and shouted down "Captain, you might want to see this, to the starboard."

Captain Kidd looked through his spyglass and saw the fleet nearing them. "It looks like a Royal Navy fleet, let's get out of here, full sail ahead, three sheets to the wind." He ordered.

Little did he know that the Royal Navy were not the only people following them, for just leaving the bay was the Black Dog, which was Blackbeard's ship, a magnificent Galleon. It seemed that someone had told him about the map. There must be a traitor on the Audacious.

"We must keep our distance so they don't see us following them" ordered Captain Blackbeard "we will go on half sail until I order otherwise."

The night was drawing in. Captain Kidd posted half a dozen guards around the ship. In the middle of the night one of the guards spotted a flickering light in the distance; he went down below to inform William. He didn't want to wake the Captain because he liked his sleep and would not be very happy being woken in the middle of the night. They went on deck and William looked through his spyglass and saw the light.

"It looks like someone is signalling." He said.

William then looked around the deck and saw a light emanating from behind one of the boats; they crept around the other side of the boat and behind the man, who was holding a lantern.

"What do you think you are doing?" Asked William, sternly.

The man turned round slowly to face William. "Jim Parker!" Said William. "Now we know why you tried to hide the map from us. You are a traitor."

"I did nothing." Said Jim Parker, trembling.

"Do not make the mistake of taking me for a fool. Who were you signalling to?" Said William.

"Nobody." Replied Jim Parker.

"You were signalling to someone, we will find out in the morning. Maybe Captain Kidd will be able to get it out of you." Said William, then turned to the guard and said. "You have done well. Now take Mr. Parker down and lock him in the brig. We will deal with him in the morning."

In the early hours of the morning, the crew awoke. William went to the Captain's quarters to see Captain Kidd and tell him about the traitor. The Captain was not too pleased.

"Where is he now?" Demanded the Captain.

"He is locked in the brig" replied William "I would have told you last night, but I thought it could wait until now."

"Bring him on deck" ordered Captain Kidd "we must make an example of him."

William went to the brig to get the traitor and bring him up on deck. Captain Kidd assembled the whole crew on deck so that everyone can see what happens to traitors; he cannot have his authority undermined.

William led the tethered man on to the main deck and the Captain stood above on the poop deck, looking down.

"You stand accused of being a traitor" said the Captain "what have you to say for yourself?"

"I did nothing wrong." Replied Jim Parker.

"You were seen signalling to someone. Who was it?" Demanded Captain Kidd.

"Nobody" replied Jim Parker "I was cold and I wanted to warm myself with my lantern."

"Is that the best excuse you have to give. It is not good enough. Do you take us for fools!" Shouted The Captain. "We know someone on another ship was signalling to you. Who was it?"

"Nobody." Said Jim Parker, adamantly.

"If you cannot find a better excuse then I have no choice but to find you guilty of treachery and sentence you to walk the plank, to be carried out immediately." Said Captain Kidd, then turned to William and ordered. "Place him on the plank."

William led him onto the plank; then with his knife, he made two cuts on the arms of Jim Parker and then nudged Mr. Parker along the plank with his sword. Jim Parker got to the end of the plank and William just put some pressure on Parker's back and he dropped into the sea below, screaming "I'm innocent!"

Moments later sharks fins appeared in the water and encircled Jim Parker who was struggling to tread water, then the sharks closed in and Jim Parker disappeared under the water, still screaming; then all of a sudden the screaming ceased and the water turned red with blood and was calm again.

"That is what happens to traitors!" Shouted Captain Kidd. "In case anyone else has any ideas." Then he ordered. "Sail on" as he turned to the bow of the ship to look onward, showing no sign of emotion.

Meanwhile, they were getting closer to the Devil's Triangle, they were just keeping ahead of the Naval fleet.

The lookout on the Audacious noticed something ahead in the distance. "Captain, look ahead, it looks like fog."

Captain Kidd looked through his spyglass. "It is fog, it looks like a real peasouper, maybe we can lose the fleet in it, they headed towards it, minutes later they entered the fog, they could see absolutely nothing, but they could hear noises, eerie noises all around them.

The sea began to turn rough and the ship started to rock from side to side. William looked over the side and saw a creature like he has never seen before. It was like a sea serpent but it must be a hundred feet long with an enormous head and long mouth which housed at least a hundred long pointed teeth.

"What in God's name is that?" William shouted, then turned to one of the men and said. "Bring me a harpoon."

The man passed the harpoon, which had a rope attached to it, to William, who took it in his hands and tried to steady himself so that he could take aim, because he only had one chance to kill the creature.

He held the harpoon over his shoulder and when he was sure of the right moment, he let it fly with all the power he had in his arms. It flew through the air and pierced the creature in its head and into its brain; then with an almighty squeal, the creature turned and shot away from the ship, taking the harpoon with it.

William noticed that the rope, which was attached to the side of the ship, began tensing up and he could not hold it and the ship started turning, being pulled by the serpent, which had immense power.

He turned to the men and shouted. "Cut the rope, cut the rope before the creature takes us down with it."

Captain Kidd ran up and with his sword, sliced straight through the rope; then with a twang it was gone and so was the serpent.

They sailed on nervously, looking around them in every direction for any further possible danger.

They were in the thick of it for about fifteen minutes, although it seemed like an eternity; then, all of a sudden it cleared. They looked around and there were mountains all around them. It was like they had entered another world.

"Where are we?" Said William, hesitantly.

"I don't know" replied Captain Kidd, looking over the map "I think we must be in the Devil's Triangle, I don't recognise any of it."

Just then they heard some piercing screams coming from behind them. Captain Kidd, William and the rest of the crew all looked round. It was coming from in the midst of the fog; Captain Kidd ordered the helmsman to go on. He noticed in front of him that there was a passage through the mountains, so they headed for it. They proceeded through the mountains with caution.

There were steep craggy rocks either side of them and some bends in it so they could not see the end of the passage.

"It looks like this is the right way, according to the map." Said Captain Kidd.

"How long is this passage?" Asked William.

"I have no idea" replied Captain Kidd "there is a bend in it, maybe we will know after we have got round the bend."

Meanwhile another ship appeared through the fog, it was Captain Meriwether on the Invincible, then seconds later the Victory appeared, with its Captain, Tom Callow. They waited a while for the other three ships of their fleet, but there was no sign of them, who knows what horrors befell them in the fog. They decided to proceed towards the passage in the mountains. If any of the other ships make it through, they will follow.

"What place is this?" Said the First Mate on the Invincible.

"I don't know" replied Captain Meriwether "I think it might be the Devil's Triangle. I thought it was a myth, but perhaps I was wrong."

Moments later, the Black Dog appeared through the fog with Captain Blackbeard at the helm, they also followed them through the mountains.

The Audacious was making headway through the mountains, it seemed like something was drawing them in. They heard strange noises which seemed to come from the rocks.

"What are those noises?" Asked William, nervously.

"I don't know" replied Captain Kidd "but I don't like it."

A shadow passed briefly over the Audacious. "What was that?" Asked William, startled.

"What?" Replied Captain Kidd, still examining the map.

"Something flew over us" he said "something big. I have a bad feeling about this place."

"I didn't see anything" said Captain Kidd "it was probably just a cloud passing."

"But there are no clouds in the sky" replied William "I have never seen a clearer sky."

"Don't get worried, William" said Captain Kidd, still with his head in the map "we are well equipped to deal with anything that is out there."

The Audacious was nearing the end of the passage, they could see the end of the mountains. They came into a clearing, it looked like another ocean and there was an island in front of them.

"Are we out of the Devil's triangle?" Asked William.

"No" replied Captain Kidd "we are in the middle of it."

Captain Kidd looked over the map again. "It looks like the treasure is on that island. There's a bay over there." He said, pointing over to the right. "We will drop anchor there for the night."

They decided to stay on their ship for the night, then start off at first light to search for the treasure, they posted several lookouts around the ship in case any danger is lurking around them.

The Invincible appeared through the mountains, followed by the Victory; they saw the Audacious anchored in the bay. "There she is Captain" said the First Mate, Charles "shall we go in?"

"No" replied Captain Meriwether "it looks like they are searching for something, we will stay back and follow them when they move, post some watchmen around the ship to let us know when they stir."

The Black Dog then appeared out of the mountains, they went to the left to keep out of sight of the Naval ships and anchored the other side of the island. It was getting dark by this time, so the were able to go by without being seen.

All night long there were eerie sound emanating from all around them. It was a nervous night for all, but luckily nothing occurred.

The next morning, the sun rose high in the sky, something was stirring on board the Audacious, Captain Kidd wanted an early start, he knew the Navy was on his heels. They lowered three boats on the blind side of the ship, then climbed down into them and rowed them ashore as quietly as possible.

The island had a sandy beach; beyond the beach there was a forest and beyond that, a range of mountains.

Once ashore, Captain Kidd and William studied the map.

"It looks like the treasure is in those mountains." Said William, pointing in their direction.

"I think you are right." Replied Captain Kidd.

They set off in that direction, not knowing that Blackbeard and his men were on their trail, they had been tipped off by the traitor on the Audacious. They hacked their way through the undergrowth with machetes, hearing a number of strange and eerie noises, but they did not see anything.

Meanwhile on board the Invincible, Captain Meriwether awoke and went on deck.

"Any sign of movement?" He asked the watchmen.

"None." One of them replied.

Captain Meriwether took out his spyglass and peered through it, scanning around the area. "Something is wrong" he said "it is too quiet".

He turned his spyglass towards the shore and saw the boats in the sand. "They're already on land!" He shouted at the lookouts "Were you lot asleep?"

He signalled to the Victory, then ordered the boats to be lowered into the sea and he and his men lowered themselves down into them. Charles Broughton stayed on board to look after the ship.

Altogether they had six boatfuls, which outnumbered both Captain Kidd and Blackbeard. They rowed to the island and left their boats on the sand, then embarked. They followed the footsteps to the end of the sand, until they reached the forest. They made their way through the forest, chopping their way through the undergrowth.

Captain Kidd and his men were nearing the end of the forest, there were still strange noises coming from the forest, noises like they have never heard before. It was endless, like someone or something was trying to scare them away.

There was movement in the trees and beady eyes peering at them, but whoever or whatever they were, it seems they are not yet ready to show themselves.

"I have a feeling we are being watched." Said William.

"It's probably just your nerves." Replied Captain Kidd.

They reached the end of the forest to a clearing. Ahead of them was a mountain.

"According to the map, the treasure is somewhere in that mountain." Said Captain Kidd.

They approached the mountain and looked around it for a way in. "Did you say in it, or on it?" Asked William, looking up the face of the mountain.

"In it" replied Captain Kidd "according to the map. Spread out and look for an entrance."

They searched up and down with no luck, then one of his men leant against one of the rocks to wipe the sweat from his forehead and he heard a grating sound emanating from the mountain. He looked round and an opening seemed to be appearing in the mountain. "Captain!" He shouted. "I think I have found it."

Captain Kidd and William raced over to see what he had found. "Well done. It looks like the entrance to a cave" said William "it's a secret doorway, we had better be aware, whoever made this may have laid some traps inside."

They proceeded to enter the cave, they lit their torches so that they could see their way ahead and advanced down what seemed to be an endless tunnel. After half an hour Captain Kidd could see the tunnel open up into a chamber in the distance and what seemed to be a light coming from it. As they neared it, they suddenly felt a crunch under foot, they looked down and saw that there were bones, human bones, strewn over the floor of the tunnel.

"I don't like the look of this" said Captain Kidd "whatever did this can't be human."

When he saw what was ahead of him he soon forgot about that, for there in front of him was a glistening mound of gold and gems, more treasures than they could ever imagine. They all rushed in, dropped their weapons to the ground and began bathing in the treasures.

"We're rich!" Shouted William.

A voice coming from the tunnel then said. "I think you'll find it is us that are rich."

It was Blackbeard and his men pointing their guns at Captain Kidd and his crew, who were unarmed because they had laid their arms down when they saw the treasure.

"Blackbeard!" Said Captain Kidd. "So you were the Pirates Jim Parker was signalling."

"Aye" replied Blackbeard. "where is the blaggard?"

"He is swimming with the sharks." Said Captain Kidd.

"That's a shame, well never mind. He did his job" said Blackbeard "just hand over the treasure."

"There is enough here for all of us, we can share it." Said Captain Kidd.

"I don't think so" replied Blackbeard "we have the guns and I have expensive tastes."

At that moment, another voice was heard from the tunnel. "I think that belongs to us" it was Captain Meriwether "lay down your arms!" He ordered.

He ordered Blackbeard and his men. "Go and stand with the other Pirates."

"Meriwether!" Exclaimed Captain Kidd.

"Do you know him?" Asked William, looking at Captain Kidd.

"Oh yes" replied Captain Kidd "we go way back."

"Enough talking." Said Meriwether and threw a large sheet over to them. "Load all of the loose treasures on the sheet and bring the chest to me." He ordered.

They carried out his orders, reluctantly; then Meriwether ordered some of his men to carry the treasure out of the cave. When they were clear, Meriwether turned to Captain Kidd and said "I owe you something Kidd" then pointed his musket at him and pulled the trigger, there was a blast and Captain Kidd fell to the ground.

"NO!" Shouted William, then knelt down at Captain Kidd's side. "He's dead. Why did you have to kill him?"

"Because he ruined my life" said Meriwether "he got me kicked out of the Navy and turned me into a drunk, just be thankful that I am letting the rest of you live."

Meriwether and the rest of his men then backed out down the tunnel and out of the cave. Once outside, he pushed the rock that opened the entrance to the cave and it closed again, trapping all the Pirates inside, then they set on their way back to their Ships.

As they reached the forest they heard noises coming from the trees, the noises seemed to be all around them and getting closer, but they could not see anyone or anything.

"What are those noises?" Said Captain Callow. "I have never heard such noises before."

"I don't know" replied Captain Meriwether "but we had better be on our guard; draw your muskets."

At that moment, spears came flying through the air, piercing some of the men, then hordes of creatures appeared out of the undergrowth from all sides bearing axes, machetes and spears. Captain Meriwether ordered his men to fire at will. The creatures were dropping like flies, but still more came.

"What manner of creatures are these?" Asked Captain Callow, whilst fighting off the creatures.

"They look like Orcs" replied Captain Meriwether "I thought they were just a myth, they are pure evil. Give them no quarter."

After half an hour of battling the creatures of hell, the creatures suddenly disappeared back into the undergrowth, leaving the battlefield strewn with dead bodies, Orcs together with Captain Meriwether's men. They would like to bury their dead but it was too dangerous. The Orcs will be back and they have to depart the hellhole as quick as possible.

"Where have they gone?" Said Captain Callow.

"I don't know" replied Captain Meriwether "but if what I have read about them is true they will be back, we must get out of here. Reload your muskets and be prepared."

They reached the edge of the forest then proceeded onto the beach and back to their boats and to their ships. Captain Meriwether had half of the treasure in his boat and the rest was in Captain Callow's boat. Captain Meriwether ordered all of the treasure to be loaded aboard his ship.

As he and his men hauled the treasures onto the deck of the Invincible, Charles Broughton stared at the treasure in awe. He was speechless for a few minutes, then he said to Captain Meriwether "what in God's name is that and where did you get it from?"

"We took it from Captain Kidd and Blackbeard." Replied Captain Meriwether.

"Where are they now?" Asked Charles.

"Captain Kidd is dead and the rest of the Pirates are trapped in a cave with no way out." Replied Captain Meriwether.

"We must take this treasure back to England" said Charles "Admiral Roswell will be pleased."

"This is not going back" said Captain Meriwether "it is payment for what the Navy did to me."

"We work for the King, we cannot keep this treasure" said Charles "if we do, then we will be no more than Pirates ourselves."

Charles drew his musket and said "I will have to relieve you of your duty and take command of this ship."

He ordered the men to take Captain Meriwether down to the brig, but only a handful of men were loyal to Charles. The rest of them were loyal to Captain Meriwether. It seems that the sight of such treasure can turn even the most honest man, with a few exceptions. It was Charles and his followers that were to occupy the brig until Meriwether decided what to do with them.

Meanwhile, back in the cave, the Pirates were looking for a way out. Luckily Captain Meriwether was concentrating on the treasure so much that it had slipped his mind to relieve them of their weapons. They proceeded down the tunnel the way they came in until they reached the entrance.

"It's blocked" said William "I can't move it. How much gunpowder have we got?" He asked.

"We all carry pouches." Replied Blackbeard.

"Empty all the pouches at the entrance; leave enough powder for one shot from each musket" said William "we will try to blow a hole in the entrance."

They poured all their powder at the foot of the entrance, then led a trail of powder a little way down the tunnel and then stood back. William drew his musket, loaded it and shot the powder to light the trail. It travelled swiftly until it reached the bulk of the powder and then there was a deafening boom as the powder ignited. It filled the tunnel with smoke. When the smoke cleared, they saw a beam of light at the end of it. It had worked, although there was only a small gap, fortunately it was large enough for everyone to dig a little more out and squeeze out through it.

William is now the Captain of the Audacious and has decided he has no choice but to join forces with Blackbeard, at least until he has his revenge on Captain Meriwether and they retrieve the treasure. He is to be known as Captain Will Morgan by his crew.

They made their way towards the forest. A little way into the forest, they came across the bodies lying all around them.

"What has happened here?" Wondered William, looking all around him. "What are these creatures?"

"They're Orcs!" Said Blackbeard, looking terrified. "They are the sons of Satan himself."

"I thought there were no such things as Orcs." Said William.

"This is the Devil's Triangle" replied Blackbeard "anything is possible here; we must be on our guard, if you see any do not hesitate to kill them because they will do much worse to you."

They continued on their way through the forest and towards the beach. Then all of a sudden their way was then blocked by a line of Orcs just standing there looking at them, brandishing evil looking weapons. They turned round to go back, but they were behind them as well; so they decided the only way out is to fight. William and his men were to take the ones in front and Blackbeard and his men were to take the Orcs behind them.

It was a fierce battle, a lot of blood was spilt; thankfully mostly from the Orcs, but both Blackbeard and William lost a few good men. It was the bloodiest battle William has ever fought.

Upon reaching the beach, they saw the HMS Invincible and Victory sailing off towards the mountain pass, then they heard a screeching noise above them, they looked up and saw a gigantic bird with a long beak and a wing span that must have been fifty feet across swooping down, just over their heads; then soaring back up into the sky and turning towards the trees, then disappeared. They all looked around them in every direction to make sure it had gone. Satisfied, they proceeded towards their boats.

The next minute it reappeared from behind the trees and swooped down again and this time it grabbed one of Blackbeard's men in it's beak, took him up in the air then shook its head similar to a dog shaking a rag doll and tossed the lifeless body into the sea, then it turned and started to swoop down again, but this time they were ready for it. They all pointed their muskets at it and when it got close enough they fired, simultaneously, bringing it down onto the beach with a thud and making the earth shake violently.

"What in God's name was that?" Said William.

"It looks like a Pterodactyl, a dinosaur" replied a bewildered Blackbeard "but their supposed to be extinct."

"That one certainly wasn't." Said William.

"It is now" replied Blackbeard "let's get out of here before we meet any more unsavoury creatures."

They went to their relevant ships, William and his men to the Audacious and Blackbeard and his men to the Black Dog, then set sail in pursuit of Captain Meriwether, who was at this moment in time at the other side of the mountains, but they are not yet out of danger, for below the surface lies another peril.

Meriwether and Callow sailed on and can now see the fog they came through a little way in the distance.

They heard an eerie sound coming from below the surface of the ocean and then all of a sudden, gigantic tentacles appeared on each side of the Victory and reached up high in the sky, then a gigantic head appeared above the side of the ship.

Captain Callow picked up a harpoon and aimed it at the creature's head, but before he could launch it, one of the tentacles came around, wrapped around the harpoon and pulled it out of the Captain's hand, then tossed it in the water; then another tentacle wrapped around his waist and squeezed the life out of him, then lifted the lifeless body up in the air and tossed it into the ocean. The creature then wrapped around the ship and pulled it into the depths, with the crew still on board.

In a few seconds the HMS Victory was gone. All Captain Meriwether and his crew could do was to watch in horror and they could not believe what they had just witnessed, so he ordered his men to be prepared and keep their eyes peeled.

"Full sail ahead" ordered Captain Meriwether "let's get out of this hell while we still can."

They sailed on through the fog and as the ship advanced, a knocking noise was heard coming from the hull, Captain Meriwether looked over the side and saw driftwood floating in the water; then he saw bodies, which looked like the remains of the Naval ships and crews that went missing on their way in.

"What on earth would have done something like this?" Said the new First Mate.

"I don't know" replied Captain Meriwether "but we had better get out of here as quick as possible.

Moments later they saw a light ahead of them and then emerged from the fog and back to the real world. When they were clear of the Devil's triangle, Captain Meriwether ordered the Charles Broughton and the other prisoners to be brought to him.

They were escorted onto the deck tethered in shackles and lined up facing Captain Meriwether.

Captain Meriwether looked down on them from the poop deck and said "have you reconsidered your decision to go against us?"

"Never" replied Charles "we will never join you traitors."

"What say the rest of you?" Said Captain Meriwether.

They all replied together "never."

"Very well" said Captain Meriwether, then ordered his men to lower one of the boats into the water.

"There is enough water and food in the boat for one day" said Captain Meriwether "you should have found land by then."

Charles and his loyal followers climbed down into the boats and started to drift away from the Invincible.

Charles turned back to the ship and shouted "you will not get away with this. I will see you hang for what you have done."

Meanwhile, the Audacious was coming through the mountains followed by the Black Dog, on the trail of Captain Meriwether. They reached the open water, they heard noises coming from below, eerie noises, like the ones heard by Captain Meriwether and his crew.

"What was that?" Said one of William's men.

"Be on your guard, men" ordered William "keep your eyes peeled."

All of a sudden the Audacious started rocking from side to side, the men had to hold fast to something to avoid being thrown overboard. Then the giant tentacles appeared all around the ship, William drew his sword and with one swing of it sliced straight through one of the tentacles. It dropped to the deck and there was an almighty ear piercing squeal, then the tentacles all disappeared below the surface, sending waves twenty feet high, lifting the Audacious above the water. After it abated the sea became calm again. William ordered his men to throw the tentacle overboard and carry on their way.

Blackbeard and his crew were watching this in horror and thanked their lucky stars it wasn't their ship being attacked, whatever it might have been.

"Let's get out of here" ordered William "before it comes back with its family."

They reached the fog, which is the edge of the triangle, they still had to be wary, at least until they get back to their own world.

The fog cleared; they have made it, but now they have lost Captain Meriwether, there was no sign of his ship. Blackbeard appeared behind them, they had made it without any mishaps.

"Thank the heavens" said William's First Mate "I never want to go there again. It was like your worst nightmare."

"Don't worry" replied William "I don't think that will be necessary."

Chapter Three
Vengeance Is Mine

The Audacious and the Black Dog sailed towards the Caribbean; they could do with a rest after all that excitement. Three days later they anchored up in the bay of Tortuga.

"You can all go ashore" said William "enjoy yourselves, you've earned it. Tomorrow we will go after Meriwether and the treasure."

They laid the gangplanks down and went ashore joined by Blackbeard and his men. They were partners in crime, at least until they recover the treasure of the Conquistadors from Captain Meriwether and William has his revenge for the cold blooded killing of his Captain and friend, Captain John Kidd.

William and Blackbeard went for a drink in the Buccaneer's Arms to discuss how they are going to find Captain Meriwether and retrieve their treasure.

A man walked through the door that was familiar to Blackbeard and sat at a table not far from them with half a dozen of his most hardened men. He was a hard looking man with long black hair, a scar on his right cheek and an eye patch over his right eye.

"See that man over there?" Said Blackbeard, pointing with his eyes. "That's Captain John Ward, the richest Pirate in these waters."

Moments later, Captain Ward walked over to their table. "Captain Blackbeard!" He exclaimed, then looked at William and asked "and who is this?"

"This is Captain William Morgan." Replied Blackbeard.

"Ah yes, I have heard of you" said Captain Ward "you were sailing with John Kidd."

"Aye that's right." Replied William.

"How is the scoundrel?" Asked Captain Ward.

"He is dead." Replied William.

"That is a shame" said Captain Ward "he was a good man. A good Pirate" then added "I heard you were looking for a ship. The Invincible." Said Captain Ward.

"Where did you hear that?" Asked Blackbeard.

"On the street" replied Captain Ward "why are you looking for it?"

"Because the Captain killed a friend of mine." Said Blackbeard.

"I didn't know you had any friends" said Captain Ward, jokingly "I thought you had killed them all."

"No, I have a few left" said Blackbeard "the friend in question is Captain Kidd."

"In that case, I will help you. Who is the Captain of the Invincible?" Asked Captain Ward.

"Meriwether, George Meriwether." Replied Blackbeard.

"I thought he was no longer in the Navy. I heard he was kicked out." Said Captain Ward, then added "He was seen sailing in a South Easterly direction. There is a group of islands in the South Atlantic, perhaps they are going there. Say hello from me when you see him and make him suffer; badly." Captain Ward then walked back to his table.

Captain Blackbeard and William finished their drinks, then two very pretty girls walked up to their table, one of them leant over and put her hands on the table revealing her cleavage, she had long red hair, piercing blue eyes and wearing a white low cut blouse with short frilled sleeves and a red knee length skirt. Her friend had long black hair and brown eyes and wearing a red dress with a black belt around her waist.

"Do you two want to have a good time?" The redhead asked, with her eyes fixed on William and making it difficult to refuse.

William just sat there with his eyes fixed on the girl's cleavage not knowing what to say. Nothing like this has ever happened to him before.

"Why not." Replied Captain Blackbeard, with his eyes on the black haired girl. "How can we refuse two such lovely busty wenches?"

They followed the girls upstairs to their rooms. Blackbeard went into a room with the black haired girl and William went into another room with the redhead. William was a bit nervous because he had never done anything like that before, but the girl would show him what to do. She sat him on the bed.

"What's your name?" She asked.

"William" he replied "William Morgan."

"I'm Rose, Rose Crowley."

"That's a pretty name." Said William.

"Thank you, now shall we get down to business?" Prompted Rose.

"Yes, I would like that." Replied William.

She started to undo the buttons on his shirt, then pulled it off, over his arms, then unbuttoned his trousers and pulled them down over his legs, then she guided his hands to her breasts and he began to fondle them gently and she began panting.

"Make love to me." She ordered.

William undid the buttons on Rose's blouse, which were at the back and removed it, then he undid the buttons on her skirt and it dropped to the floor, then Rose stepped out of it. William removed the rest of her clothes, got on top of her and started making love to her. They were writhing in a passionate embrace and were both making sounds of pleasure which could be heard in the next room.

After they had finished, William rolled over on the bed, exhausted.

"That was nice." He said.

"For me too." Replied Rose.

"We will do this again next time I am here." Said William.

"I would like that" replied Rose "that will cost two pieces of silver."

"Do I have to pay for it?" Asked William, taken aback.

"It is my job" said Rose "I have to live!"

"Very well" said William "it was worth it."

William and Rose exited the room at the same time as Blackbeard came out of his.

"Did you enjoy that?" Asked Blackbeard.

"Yes." Replied William.

"I thought you might have" said Blackbeard "we could hear you."

They then went down to have a drink or two. Rose and the other girl joined them at their table.

"We have to get back to our ships soon." Said William.

"Can I come with you?" Rose begged.

"No" replied William "a Pirate's life is not for you."

"I have nothing here" said Rose "all I am here for is to please men. I can look after myself; my Father taught me how to fight."

"It is bad luck to have women on a ship." Said William, trying to dissuade her.

"I'm not superstitious." said Rose.

"No, but my men are. I will have to put it to them." Replied William.

"You are the Captain, are you not?" Said Rose.

"I am" replied William "but without the respect of your men you will always be looking over your shoulder, wary of a mutiny."

When they had finished, they went back to their ships. William took Rose along. They boarded the Audacious and the crew were on deck. As soon as Rose stepped on board, the air was deafening with the sound of whistles and cheers. That answered William's question.

William and Blackbeard went down to William's cabin, where he pulled out some charts of the South Atlantic. They studied them carefully, looking for the islands that Captain Ward mentioned so that they can plot a course for the morning.

"These must be the islands." Said William, pointing to a spot on the map.

"You could be right" replied Blackbeard "it looks like they are about three days sailing from here."

In the morning, they got their supplies and replenished their armouries and then set sail, bearing South East.

On the third day into their voyage from Tortuga, the lookout cried from the crow's nest on the Audacious. "Land Ahoy!"

William took out his spyglass and saw a group of islands in front of them, but no sign of Captain Meriwether's ship, the Invincible. All of a sudden, he saw a sail appear from behind the rocks on the west island. As it emerged from the rocks, he saw that it was indeed the Invincible.

William kept his spyglass to his eye and in the direction of the Invincible, but they were also being watched, for there was Captain Meriwether looking at them through his spyglass.

"Pirates!" He cried. "Full sail ahead. Man the guns."

They must try to outrun the Pirates, for they are no match for two fully armed ships, but if they must, they will have to be prepared to fight.

The Invincible was a fast ship so it was not going to be easy to catch them, but William had a few tricks up his sleeve.

William saw them trying to make a run for it, so he signalled to Captain Blackbeard to cut them off and go around them. As the Audacious neared the Invincible, William gave the order to face them broadside. Captain Blackbeard gave the same order from his ship, which was the other side of the Invincible.

"Man the guns" he ordered "prepare to fire."

"Fire!" William ordered.

"Fire!" Ordered Captain Meriwether.

"Fire!" Ordered Captain Blackbeard.

The air was full of cannon fire and smoke, not a lot could be seen. When the smoke cleared, it was evident that there was a lot of damaged incurred to all the vessels and a lot of crewmen dead, on all sides. William and Blackbeard each ordered their crews to board the Invincible. They led their men over on ropes.

"Captain Meriwether is mine." William ordered.

As they landed on the deck of the Invincible, Captain Meriwether's men were waiting for them. They drew their swords and muskets and a fierce battle ensued. William was fighting his way through, looking for Captain Meriwether, until he saw him on the poop deck, crossing swords with Blackbeard. It was a hard fought battle and then Captain Meriwether lunged at Blackbeard and thrust his sword through Blackbeard's chest. Blackbeard reeled back, clutching his chest and dropped to the ground, fatally wounded and then Captain Meriwether walked up to him to finish him off. He looked down at Captain Blackbeard, then pointed his sword at him and thrust it straight through Blackbeard's heart, whose head then dropped to the side.

William swung up to the poop deck with his legs outstretched and headed straight for Captain Meriwether. He caught him with both feet and sent him flying back against the side of the ship and then William landed on the deck, sword in hand.

Captain Meriwether stood up with his sword held aloft and William faced him brandishing his sword.

"Now you will pay for killing my Captain and friend." Said William.

"He deserved it" replied Meriwether "he ruined my life."

"Now I will end it." Said William.

"So be it." Replied Captain Meriwether.

They crossed swords and then began to fight. William lunged at Meriwether, who blocked him, then Meriwether lunged at William, who dodged it to the right, then slashed Meriwether's sword down, then William lifted his foot and pushed Meriwether back. He fell to the ground, picked up his sword and stood up, then they crossed their swords again in a stalemate, trying to push each other back, then William pushed Meriwether up against the side of the ship, they were still in a stalemate, then William pulled a dagger out and thrust it into Meriwether's gut, whose face then turned distorted in agony. He then fell back off the side of the ship and into the sea below.

"That is for Captain Kidd." Said William.

His revenge is complete, Captain Meriwether is dead.

William went over to Blackbeard to see how he was, but to no avail; He too was dead. William looked onto the main deck of the ship and saw a lot of bodies strewn around it. All of Meriwether's men seemed to be dead along with a lot of William's and Blackbeard's men. The men still standing looked towards William.

"Captain Meriwether is dead!" shouted William, then continued "and so too is Captain Blackbeard. If any of Blackbeard's men want to join us, they will be welcome."

They all shouted. "Aye, Captain."

"Very well" said William "let us get the treasure and depart this place."

They searched the Invincible inside and out, but there was no sign of the treasure, so they deduced that Meriwether must have buried it on the west island where they emerged from, just then one of William's men came from below holding a knife to another man's throat.

"Look what I found hiding below" he said "a coward."

William walked up to the man and said. "It looks like you are the only survivor; so you are going to tell us where you buried our treasure."

"I don't know." Said the man.

"Don't take us for fools!" Shouted William. "You will tell us or suffer the consequences."

"I don't know" repeated the man "I stayed on the ship when they went to the island."

"I don't believe you." Said William, then said to his First Mate. "Take him over to the Audacious; we will deal with him later."

They went back to their ships, then fired some shots into the hull of the Invincible and watched as it sank to the bottom of the Ocean. They then started to sail to the west island to search for the treasure.

William told his First Mate to bring the prisoner to him, which he did without delay.

"Now you are going to tell me where the treasure is buried." He said to the prisoner.

"I told you I don't know." Replied the prisoner, shaking in his boots.

"Very well; if you persist in lying to me you will pay the price." Said William, then turned to his First Mate and said "Bring me a long length of strong rope, we will keelhaul him until he tells us."

The First Mate brought a length of rope, tied one end around the prisoner and the other end he tied to the spar on the bow of the ship.

"This is your last chance to save your life." Shouted William.

"I don't know anything!" Screamed the prisoner.

"Throw him over." Ordered William.

The First Mate pushed the prisoner who then dived into the sea below, then he got dragged by the current under the keel of the ship, screaming. This went on for a few minutes, then all of a sudden the screaming ceased and there was silence. The crew looked over the sides of the ship and saw a slick of blood. They pulled the rope back up and the body of the prisoner came up with it, torn to pieces.

"He didn't know anything, throw him back in" ordered William "let the sharks have him."

They continued to the west island and when they arrived there they put four boatfuls ashore, which should be enough to comb the island. They searched every square foot of the island, but there was no sign of the treasure, so William decided to stop searching and go to get their ships repaired and maybe return another day. It will still be there, since anyone who knew where it was is dead; so they set sail back to Tortuga.

Admiral Roswell heard the news about his old friends, Captain George Meriwether and Charles Broughton and decided that if you want a job done properly you have to do it yourself; so he decided to travel down to Portsmouth and commandeer two fully armed ships of war to go after the Pirates.

Admiral Roswell took charge of the HMS. Vanquish, then met the Captain of the HMS. Courageous; Captain James Gordon.

"You are coming with me to bring some Pirates to justice." Admiral Roswell ordered Captain Gordon.

"Who are we going after?" Asked Captain Gordon.

"Captain Blackbeard and Captain Kidd." The Admiral replied, not knowing that they were dead. "We will set sail at first light."

The sun was rising on the horizon, the decks of the Vanquish and the Courageous started filling up. Admiral Roswell showed his face on deck and gave the order to set sail for the Caribbean. It will be a long and arduous journey, but it has to be done. Someone has to stop these Pirates.

Admiral Roswell has had a long career in the Navy and spent most of it at sea on the front line, so he is a very experienced sailor.

On the third day at sea, dark clouds are seen ahead of them.

"It looks like a storm is ahead" said Admiral Roswell "take down the sails, batten down the hatches" he ordered "hold on tight, it is going to be a big one."

Ahead of them were waves reaching up thirty feet at least; then it hit them. It was like coming up against a brick wall, waves lashed over the deck, sweeping away anything that wasn't held down. The ships were rocking from side to side at almost a ninety degree angle. The helmsman was struggling with the wheel, trying to stay on course while the waves battered him constantly.

It was no good giving orders because nobody could hear anything through the noise of the wind and rain that was continuously attacking their vessels. Everyone must carry out their duty to ensure they get out of it in one piece.

Minutes later the storm subsided and they had to assess the damage done to both the Vanquish and the Courageous. Amazingly there was not as much damage done that had been expected. At least the decks did not need swabbing and all the men were present and correct. They continued on their way to fight a more fearsome battle.

The next day was a complete contrast to the prior day. The sun was beating down on the decks of the HMS. Vanquish and Courageous. Admiral Roswell was standing at the bow of his ship looking out to sea.

The lookout spotted something in the distance and shouted. "Land ahoy!"

Admiral Roswell took out his spyglass and placed it to his eye and spotted some figures on the beach. They moved in closer, as close as they could without grounding.

"They're men in naval uniform" said Admiral Roswell, then ordered "lower the boats. We will go ashore and find out who they are."

They lowered three boats into the water; then climbed down into them, leaving room for the people on the island to be picked up, then rowed to the island. Upon reaching the island, they dragged the boats onto the sand and were greeted by half a dozen dishevelled men, all with long straggly beards.

Admiral Roswell took a closer look at one of them, who looked familiar to him and said "don't I know you?"

"I am Charles Broughton" said the man "you don't know how good it is to see you, Admiral."

"Charles?" Said the Admiral "I was told you were dead" then added "what of Captain Meriwether?" Thinking that if Charles is alive, then so to is Captain Meriwether. Maybe the reports of their deaths were false.

"He is a traitor" replied Charles "he has become nothing more than a Pirate."

"How did you get here?" Asked the Admiral.

"Meriwether put us afloat in a boat" said Charles "but our boat got battered in a storm and we ended up here."

"We must get you back to the ship and get you cleaned up" said the Admiral "then we will go after the traitor."

They got back aboard the Vanquish and set sail again. Now they have another foe to contend with in Captain Meriwether.

They were at sea for another two days when a shout came from the crow's nest. "Two ships on the starboard bow, Admiral!"

Admiral Roswell took out his spyglass and scanned the horizon; then his gaze became fixed on the ships in question. He could just make out the name on one of the ships, 'The Audacious'.

"That's who we are looking for" said the Admiral, then shouted down to the gunnery "man the guns and prepare to fire on my order."

The Admiral then turned to face the crew to give the orders to advance.

"Full sail ahead" he ordered "let's finish this, then we can concentrate on finding the traitor before we go home."

Admiral Roswell was too sure of himself. This was not going to be an easy fight as many before them know only too well.

Captain William Morgan was ready for them. He spotted them a long way out, so he had plenty of time to prepare to engage them. They split up, the Audacious went one way and the Black Dog, the other way. This will separate the Naval ships, so it will be easier to defeat them.

The Admiral's vessel, 'HMS. Vanquish' followed the Audacious and Captain Gordon's ship, 'HMS. Courageous' went after the Black Dog.

After they had achieved their objective of separating the Naval ships, William ordered his gunners to load their guns and prepare to fire on his order, then ordered his helmsman to turn hard to port and face the Vanquish broadside, which they did.

"Fire!" William shouted, and a loud blast went out as all the portside guns fired simultaneously.

"Fire!" Ordered Admiral Roswell, as his ship was being ripped apart. He had lost half of his starboard guns now.

"Reload, then fire at will." Ordered William, which they did to great effect.

After the second salvo, there was much damage done to the Vanquish and William decided to board her. He ordered his men to follow as he swung over to the vessel, ensued by the whole crew of the Audacious.

William was the first to land on the deck of the Vanquish, sword in hand ready to strike out at anyone who gets close to him. He was scanning the deck for the Captain of the ship.

He noticed a man at the bow of the ship wearing a tricorn hat, which was Admiral Roswell, so he fought his way up the steps and was face to face with the Admiral.

"Where is Captain Kidd?" The Admiral asked.

"He is dead" replied William "Captain Meriwether killed him. He shot him in cold blood."

"At least he did something right." Said the Admiral.

"Do you mean to say that you ordered Meriwether to kill my Captain?" Asked William.

"Yes, and who are you?" Asked the Admiral.

"I am Captain William Morgan. The man who is going to take your life." Said William.

"You had better be good with that weapon." Replied Admiral Roswell.

"I was good enough to get the better of your Captain Meriwether." Said William.

"So the reports of Meriwether's demise were true." Said the Admiral.

"Very much so." Replied William.

"That saves me a job pursuing the traitor." Said the Admiral.

"Why do you think you will be able to go after anyone" said William "you will not be alive much longer."

They crossed swords; the Admiral lifted his up and took a swipe, William blocked it, then took a swipe himself across the Admiral's chest and the Admiral blocked that, then they crossed swords again across their bodies, trying to push each other backwards.

"You fight well." Said Admiral Roswell.

"I had a good teacher." Replied William.

They stayed in that pose for a few minutes, each trying to gain the advantage, then something caught the Admiral's eye and he looked away for a split second. That gave William his opportunity; he pushed the Admiral from him and lunged his sword into the Admiral's stomach. Admiral Roswell stared William in the eye with a grimace on his face, then fell back onto the deck and his head fell to the side. William knelt down beside him and felt for a pulse; there was none. The Admiral was dead.

William descended down the steps onto the main deck. The fight had subsided and all of the crew of the HMS. Vanquish were dead. William ordered his crew back onto the Audacious.

Back on board, they went in search of the Black Dog. They found it and it seemed that they were not so fortunate. All that could be seen of it were the masts protruding from the water. It was sunk along with the HMS. Courageous.

William ordered his crew to turn and head back to Tortuga for a long deserved rest and recuperation.

Chapter Four
The Story Of Van Helsing

Born on 18th June 1779 in Rotterdam, Holland, Robert Van Helsing was an only son. His parents, Edward and Katherine brought him to England in 1786 when he was very young, they settled in the port of Southampton.

His Mother, Katherine was an attractive woman, tall and slim; she had long black hair put up in a bun. Edward, his Father was a well built man with short dark hair and sideburns.

They lived in a big detached house with three bedrooms. The front door opened into a tiled hallway with a staircase in the middle. On the left was the living room, next to that was the study, and on the other side of the staircase were the dining room and the kitchen. The staircase rose up to a landing which led to the bedrooms and the bathroom. On the left were the master bedroom which had a large four poster bed and a long dresser with a large mirror attached to it, and the second bedroom was on the right of it, on the right of that was the bathroom with a tub sitting in the centre of the room and on the right of that was the third bedroom.

Outside, at the rear of the house in the garden there were two apple trees and a pear tree, also a barn, which Edward was using for his work; he had converted it into a forge.

He was a silversmith by trade and was good at his job; he set up a business with the money he had earned in his native Holland. He made all sorts of items for the nobility there, as well as for the middle classes and it wasn't long before he made a name for himself in England.

He put Robert into a decent school, where he did well; he was a bright young lad and he turned out to be a star pupil.

As he was growing up, he developed a yen for the sea and had a fascination with ships; he would always walk to the docks after school and at weekends to watch the ships coming in and out of the docks, he came to know every type of ship that came in, thinking that maybe one day he would be on board one of those ships, sailing the high seas in search of adventure.

When he was sixteen years of age, Robert enlisted in His Majesty's Navy, he had turned into a handsome young man, he was tall with broad shoulders, dark hair and brown eyes.

He started off as a cabin boy on the 'HMS Dauntless', an A1 fully equipped Frigate under Captain Will Douglas, doing odd jobs, but he was a good worker and so eager to learn that it wasn't long before he got promoted to deckhand, then Midshipman within a year.

He was being taught how to fight using guns, knives and swords and by any means necessary. He was a quick learner and within a few months he was keeping up with the best on board. He was soon to become an expert in the art of swordplay.

His first commission under Captain Douglas was to join the fleet at Portsmouth headed by Admiral Beecham and sail to engage the French fleet in battle, which was spotted off the coast of Dover.

Their fleet consisted of four Men of War, three Galleons and five Frigates, of which the HMS Dauntless was one.

They received the orders to set sail for Dover. Their sails went up and they headed east for Dover with Admiral Beecham leading the way. There was a strong tail wind, so it didn't take them long to get there.

When they reached the English Channel, the French fleet were in view. Captain Douglas peered through his spyglass for a closer look.

"There must be twenty warships at least." He said.

The French must have seen them, because they started moving, so Admiral Beecham then gave the order to fan out in formation. He also gave the order to man the guns and to prepare to fire on his order.

When they came within range, they all turned to port so that they were broadside of the French fleet. The order came to fire and all of the guns on all of the ships of the fleet fired in unison, then the French returned the fire, the Royal Naval fleet reloaded and fired another salvo of shots into the French fleet, but the whole area was immersed in smoke; not much could be seen, so they just had to guess where the enemy ships were.

When the smoke cleared, they could see the extent of the damage to the enemy and to their fleet. Half of the French fleet was on its way down to Davy Jones locker and most of the ships still afloat had extensive damage.

The Royal Navy had lost three ships and some of the others had masts down and gaping holes blasted in their sides. It was utter carnage. Robert had never seen anything like it before, but being in His Majesty's Navy, he was certain to see it again. Many people were dead and many ships sunk and badly damaged.

After a long and bloody battle, the French fleet turned to retreat and Admiral Beecham ordered his fleet to follow them for a few miles to make sure they leave English waters. Once they were, he ordered his fleet back to Portsmouth.

On the 14th June 1799; Captain Douglas and his crew were commissioned to go after Pirates, namely one Captain William Morgan and his motley crew that were terrorising the Atlantic Ocean and bring them to book.

They were wanted for high piracy and for the murder of Captain Meriwether and Admiral Roswell as well as the crews of their ships.

After filling up with supplies and ammunition, they set sail from Southampton, heading west across what could be treacherous waters.

Four days on and they had reached the middle of the Atlantic, heading towards America, when a shout was heard from the crows nest. " SHIP AHOY!"

Captain Douglas took out his spyglass and looked through it. He saw that it was a Galleon with the name 'Audacious' on its bow. It never had any colours flying, so they could not be sure who it was, but they were not going to take any chances.

"Full sail ahead" ordered Captain Douglas "be aware of anything suspicious."

"Aye aye Captain." Replied the First Mate.

"Load the guns" ordered the Captain "when we get close enough, we will see if they acknowledge us, if not, fire one off her bow."

They pulled alongside the Audacious and then all of a sudden a flag went up. It was the Jolly Roger, they were Pirates. The Audacious fired upon them; a blast ripped a hole in the side of the Dauntless. They fired back, taking down the centre mast of the Pirate ship.

Under cover of the smoke, Captain Douglas took two dozen men including Robert to storm the Audacious, swinging over on ropes. Robert was not afraid to get into the action; this is a chance to put what he learnt into practice. He was fighting like a man possessed. All that was heard were swords clattering and the sound of gunfire.

Captain Douglas spotted their Captain on the poop deck and slowly walked up the steps. The Captain had his back towards Captain Douglas.

"Captain." Called Captain Douglas.

The Captain turned round as if in slow motion to face Captain Douglas.

"Well, well" said captain Douglas "if it isn't Captain Will Morgan. What a prize."

"Hello Douglas" said Captain Morgan, lifting his sword aloft "if you want to take me, you will have to kill me, so let's see what you have got."

They crossed their swords then began to fight. Morgan lunged at Douglas and Douglas blocked, then Douglas lunged at Morgan and Morgan blocked; then Douglas took a swipe across Morgan's chest, slashing his shirt and drawing a little blood. Morgan looked down at his chest, then raised his sword above his head and brought it down with some force, but Douglas was prepared for this so he held his sword up to protect himself and Morgan's sword clattered on top of Douglas's, then Douglas swept it away from him, then knocked it out of Morgan's hand and held his sword up to Morgan's throat, almost breaking the skin. Captain Morgan stared into Captain Douglas's eyes with no sign of emotion, almost like he was dead inside.

"Do it" said William Morgan, almost goading him into it, then added "if you can."

Robert looked up and saw what looked like Captain Douglas about to kill Captain Morgan and shouted. "Captain, no. It's all over, we have won. We must take him back to stand trial."

Captain Douglas looked down and said. "You are right Robert. Killing him will be too quick and easy."

Captain Douglas grabbed Morgan by the shirt, then tossed him down the steps and ordered. "Take them to the Audacious, they will go back and hang for their crimes."

Many Pirates were killed that day. Captain Douglas lost a dozen good men. They took the surviving Pirates as prisoners, including their Captain, William Morgan and then they headed for home. Robert and a handful of men stayed on the Pirate ship to sail it back home.

They had a tailwind behind them, so it was plain sailing for them. Four days of sailing and they were pulling into Southampton harbour. Their ship needed some repairs done while they were on shore. They loaded the captives into a prison cart to take them to the Admiralty in London.

"Can I visit my parents before we go to London?" Asked Robert.

"Certainly, I think you've deserved it, but we have to get these prisoners to London as soon as possible, so you can come later and meet us there" said the Captain "we will be staying at the Black Swan Inn, near Admiralty Arch."

Robert got to his parents house, went in and was greeted with a hug from his Mother, Katherine, who was just relieved that he had come back alive and his Father was happy he was back too.

"I can't stay too long, I have to go to London to be with my crew, but I will come back as soon as I can." Said Robert.

"You must at least stay for dinner" said Katherine "I have a big turkey cooking in the oven."

"How can I resist my favourite bird?" replied Robert. "Very well."

Robert stayed for a sumptuous turkey dinner with potatoes, home grown vegetables and a delicious gravy, and for afters, a delicious home made apple pie made with their own apples, then he stayed for the night.

He sat up until late having a man to man chat with his Father. Robert told his Father about his exploits on the high seas and about catching the fearsome Pirate Captain Will Morgan, who had been so allusive for all these years.

Edward fetched a bottle of whiskey from the drinks cabinet. He placed two glasses on the table and half filled them, then passed one of them to Robert.

"Here Robert" he said "let us drink to your future as a Pirate hunter."

They lifted their glasses up and downed their drinks, which made Robert almost choke. This was the first time Robert had drank Whiskey.

His Father patted his back and said "You'll be alright son. You will get used to it."

At first light Robert said his goodbyes and then left for London. He met up with Captain Douglas; he was at the Black Swan Inn having some ale with some of his crew members. Robert got a jug of ale and sat down with the men.

"Admiral Calderdale would like to see you tomorrow at noon." Said Captain Douglas.

"What for?" Asked Robert, looking worried.

"I don't know" replied Captain Douglas "you will have to ask him when you see him."

"By the way" said Robert "what did you do with the prisoners?"

"They are in jail at the Admiralty, awaiting trial." Replied Captain Douglas.

The next day Robert went to the Admiralty. It was a huge building, three storeys high in the shape of a square with a courtyard in the middle of it, which was used as a training ground.

He went up to the office of Admiral Calderdale and sat in the reception room. A beautiful slim young lady walked in, she had long blond hair, green eyes and long legs, she sat down next to Robert and they got talking to each other, it was clear they liked each other, even after such a short time.

"My name is Robert." He said, sheepishly.

"I am Annabelle" she replied "what are you here for?"

"I have been summoned by Admiral Calderdale" replied Robert "I don't know why."

The Admiral's door opened and out stepped a stout distinguished, smart dressed man in uniform with white hair and beard. He was quite short, with a scar on his left cheek.

"Robert Van Helsing?" He called out.

"That's me." Replied Robert.

"Can you come through?" Ushered the Admiral.

Robert nervously went through the door into the Admiral's office, not knowing what to expect.

"Take a seat" said the Admiral, ushering him to a leather armchair at his desk "I am Admiral John Calderdale. I have asked you here because I have heard good things about you from Captain Douglas. I have decided to promote you to First Mate under Captain Douglas on the HMS Dauntless. Will you accept the commission?"

"I will be delighted" said Robert, almost unbelieving of what he just heard "I can't think of a better Captain to serve."

"Good! Your commission will start with immediate effect. That will be all, by the way my daughter needs to go home, can you escort her, make sure she gets home safely."

"It would be my honour" said Robert "where is she?"

"She is outside in the reception room." The Admiral replied.

"Is Annabelle your daughter?" He enquired.

"Have you already met her?" Asked the Admiral.

"Yes" replied Robert "we met in your reception area, it would be my pleasure to escort her home."

"Straight home!" The Admiral said, harshly.

A good chance for romance to blossom, for as soon as they saw each other in the reception room, they knew they were drawn to each other, you might say it was love at first sight.

They left the Admiralty. Robert hailed a hansom cab, he helped Annabelle up into it and then he climbed in. They took the scenic route to her house, they had a good talk and they knew they were right for each other.

"Your Father has just made me First Mate on the Dauntless. Maybe one day I will be Captain and have my own ship." Said Robert.

"I am pleased for you" said Annabelle, then added "that means you'll be mostly at sea."

He could see that she was a bit upset, although they had only just met.

"Can I see you again?" asked Robert.

"Come for me tomorrow morning" said Annabelle "perhaps we can take a walk together."

Robert left. He went to meet Captain Douglas and a few more of the men in the Black Swan Inn. He told the Captain about his commission.

"I know" said Captain Douglas "he asked me for my advice and I told him."

"You said you didn't know what he wanted with me." Said Robert.

"I know. I didn't want to spoil the surprise." Replied Captain Douglas.

"Thank you." Said Robert.

"Not at all, you have earned it." The Captain replied.

"I am also taking his daughter out tomorrow." Robert said, with a smile on his face.

"Do you think that is wise?" Said Captain Douglas. "What if things go wrong?"

"It will be alright, we are only going for a walk" said Robert "she is going to show me around the streets of London."

"Very well" said Captain Douglas "but be very careful, I know Admiral Calderdale. He loves his Daughter very much and if any one hurts her, he will spare them no mercy."

"I will keep that in mind, but I have no intention to hurt her." Said Robert.

They carried on drinking until late, then turned in for the night.

The next morning, Robert went to pick up Annabelle. The door was answered by the butler, The Admiral was there. He has a butler, cook and maid to look after him and Annabelle. He lived in a large terraced house in Kensington, there were steps rising up to the front door, inside there was a hall with a magnificent chandelier hanging down from the high ceiling, on the right of the hall, a large living/dining room, on the left of that a large kitchen. On the left of the hall was a winding staircase leading to three bedrooms and the bathroom, under the staircase was a door with steps descending down to a wine cellar. Admiral Calderdale was a wine connoisseur.

"Are you two going out?" Asked the Admiral.

"Yes" said Robert "we are just going for a walk. Is Mrs. Calderdale not here, I would very much like to meet her?"

"No, she died three years ago. It has just been Annabelle and I since, that's why I am so protective of her." Replied the Admiral.

"Sorry to hear that." Said Robert.

"Now go and enjoy yourselves." Said the Admiral.

They left and went for a walk around Hyde Park; they sat on a bench and just talked. They had fallen in love. Robert was going to make the most of his leave by seeing as much as he could of Annabelle.

"The Marriage of Figaro is playing at the Royal Opera House tonight. It's a new opera by Mozart, do you want to go with me?" Asked Robert.

"I would love to" replied Annabelle "I like Opera."

"Good, I will pick you up at 7.00 o'clock tonight." Said Robert.

Robert walked Annabelle home, and then he went back to the Inn where he was staying. Annabelle went into her house; her Father was there, sitting in the living room in front of an open fire.

"Did you have a good time?" Asked the Admiral.

"Yes Father, we had a good talk, I think I am in love" replied Annabelle "he is taking me to the Opera tonight."

"That's nice, he seems like a nice man but you have just met him. Just make sure you don't get hurt, you know he is going to be at sea for a long time." Said the Admiral.

"I know, but I love him and I will wait for him." Annabelle replied.

"You really have grown into a mature and sensible woman." Said the Admiral.

7.00 o'clock came, there was a knock at the door, Admiral Calderdale answered it and it was Robert, looking very handsome in his uniform.

"Good evening, Admiral" said Robert "I've come to pick Annabelle up, we are going to the Opera."

"I know" said the Admiral "she told me. Look after her, she is all I have got."

"I won't let anything happen to her, don't worry." Said Robert.

Annabelle glided down the stairs, she looked stunning. She was wearing a long flowing red dress with matching red shoes, a gorgeous pearl necklace and a red carnation in her hair. Robert stared at her open mouthed.

"You look beautiful!" Exclaimed Robert.

"Thank you." Replied Annabelle.

They went to say goodnight to her Father, then headed for the door.

"Goodnight, enjoy yourselves." Said the Admiral.

They arrived at the Royal Opera House, went in and sat in the dress circle. There were programmes on the seats, so Robert picked his up and started to read all about the opera in question.

"It says here that it is based on a play by a man named Beaumarchais that was stopped in Vienna." Stated Robert.

"Why?" Asked Annabelle.

"Because it made fun of their aristocracy." Replied Robert.

"What is this opera about?" Asked Annabelle.

"It is about two servants preparing to get married; Figaro and Susanna" said Robert "but their master wants the bride-to-be for himself so he plots against Figaro. It follows on from the Barber of Seville."

The lights went down and the curtain opened. It was about to start, so they got comfortable and watched the Opera, it was a long one.

It was an opera in four acts and after the second act came an interval, so they proceeded to the bar, where two complimentary glasses of champagne were handed to them by a waiter, which Robert took in each hand, then passed one to Annabelle.

Robert raised his glass to Annabelle and said "here's to us, may we have many more nights like this?"

They clinked their glasses together, then took a sip of their champagne, whilst looking each other in the eye. The usher then entered the bar and called out "time please!"

It was time to rejoin the opera, so they sat down again to enjoy the second half.

After the opera was finished they agreed that it was the best day of their lives so far and hopefully there would be plenty more.

"Did you enjoy that?" Robert asked Annabelle.

"Very much so" replied Annabelle "even though it was in Italian and I could not understand them. The music was excellent and the plot easy to follow. Thank you for a lovely evening."

"It was entirely my pleasure" Replied Robert "I hope we can do this again sometime soon."

"I would like that very much." Said Annabelle with a big smile on her face.

Robert had to leave the next morning to go to his ship, so this was the last night until his next leave. He walked Annabelle back home and said his goodbyes. Annabelle grabbed his arm.

"I don't want you to go!" She cried.

"I must" he said "it is my duty; but don't worry, I won't be gone long."

With that, he gave her a big kiss and they hugged each other for a few minutes, then walked away, looking back and waving at Annabelle until he was out of sight.

He got back to the Black Swan Inn, and then went to bed. It was going to be a long day tomorrow.

Dawn broke; there was a knock at his door.

A voice shouted. "Are you awake, sleepy head? It's time to join our ship." It was Captain Douglas.

Robert jumped up with a start "what time is it?" He cried out.

"Six o'clock!" Shouted Captain Douglas.

Robert got dressed, had a wash in the basin and proceeded downstairs.

Captain Douglas looked at Robert, who was looking like death warmed up and said "what happened to you. Are you feeling alright?"

"I just had a late night" replied Robert "we went to the opera."

Captain Douglas replied. "If this is what women do to you, you had better leave them alone."

They went on their way back to Southampton. Robert stopped at his parents' house before going back to the ship, to tell them the news.

"Hello Mother, hello Father, I have some good news," said Robert "I have just been promoted to First Mate on the Dauntless."

"Well done, son" said his Father "I am proud of you."

"So am I." Said his Mother.

"There is another thing, I have met a woman and we are in love." Said Robert.

His parents looked at each other, stunned, and both said together "we are pleased for you."

"What is she like, is she nice?" His Mother asked.

"Yes, she is very nice and very beautiful, she is the Admiral's daughter, I will bring her here to meet you sometime. I must join my ship now, so I will have to say goodbye." Said Robert, then he departed.

Back on board the Dauntless, it is business as usual, he has to try to put Annabelle out of his mind for now and concentrate on the job at hand.

"Anchors aweigh" shouted Captain Douglas "full sail ahead."

They headed in a westerly direction, towards America.

Two days out at sea, there were dark clouds ahead.

"Looks like we may be in for a storm" said Captain Douglas to Robert "all hands on deck, batten down the hatches." He ordered.

Sure enough they ran into a storm, and it was a fierce one, it threw their ship around from side to side, the whole crew were on deck trying to keep the ship upright, it seemed to last forever, then, all of a sudden, it was over, they had weathered it without casualties and miraculously only minor damage to the ship.

Apart from the storm; it was an eventless tour of duty. No Pirates to be seen anywhere so they headed back to port. It was coming up to Christmas so the crew were not that disappointed; maybe they can spend Christmas and New Year with their loved ones and see in the new Century and hopefully a new, peaceful era.

Back in port; Everyone went to their own homes and to their families, those that had families.

Robert went to his parents' house and they were pleased to see him. They had purchased an enormous Christmas tree, which they had decorated to the hilt. This tree took up a whole corner of the Living room.

Two weeks to go until Christmas is upon them and Robert received a telegram from the Admiralty. He nervously opened it, thinking the worst, that he might have to return to his ship for another call of duty, but it said that he was requested to visit Admiral Calderdale on the 19th December at 1200 hours at the Admiralty.

The day came and there was a knock at the door; it was Captain Douglas, who had also been summoned to the Admiralty.

"Do you know what this is about?" Asked Robert.

"I have no idea" replied Captain Douglas "I have the same telegram as you."

They took a carriage to London and entered the Admiralty and up to Admiral Calderdale's office.

"Hello men, it's nice to see you" said the Admiral "I have summoned you here because I have new orders for you."

Both Captain Douglas and Robert looked at each other, then looked at Admiral Calderdale. He could see that they were a bit nervous about what he was going to say.

"Relax" he said, assuringly "I have here your new orders, but they do not come into effect until the new year."

Captain Douglas and Robert both let out a sigh of relief.

"Something strange has been happening in the South Atlantic and I would like you to investigate it." Said the Admiral.

"When are we to set off on this mission?" Asked Captain Douglas.

"On the 4th January" came the reply from the Admiral "now you are dismissed."

Captain Douglas and Robert turned to walk out and Admiral Calderdale called to Robert and said. "Before you go, Robert; there is someone here to see you."

Annabelle walked into the room and Robert's face lit up as if he had already had all of his Christmas presents at once. She approached him and gave him a big hug, which almost squeezed the life out of him.

They just stood there in an embrace for a few minutes, kissing and squeezing; then the Admiral opened his mouth. "Can you do that outside please. I am getting a bit nauseous."

They exited the office and the Admiralty, then went for a long walk along the Thames hand in hand, sitting occasionally on a bench in each others arms just looking out over the river, wondering what the future holds for the two of them.

After a couple of hours, Robert walked Annabelle home and went in with her.

"My Father has told me to invite you over for Christmas and the New Year." Said Annabelle.

"I would like that" replied Robert "but I think my Parents would like me there at Christmas, although I could come for the new year celebrations."

"I would like that." Said Annabelle, a little disappointed because she wants Robert all for herself.

"I could stay for a few nights now if you would like." Said Robert.

The Admiral let Robert stay for as long as he liked. He put him up in the guest room.

They enjoyed their time together for that short time, then Robert had to go back home; otherwise his Parents would be upset. You can't please everyone all of the time.

Christmas morning came and Robert awoke. It was a crisp morning; he looked out of the window and snow was falling on the ground. The whole of the garden was white.

Robert was a happy man, he had everything he could want. A loving family, a beautiful girlfriend who may one day become his wife and a job he enjoys very much.

After having his wash and getting dressed, he sauntered downstairs to the wonderous smell of Christmas cooking. His Mother had bought a large goose from the market. He wandered into the living room and his Father was sitting in his armchair.

"Good morning Robert and Merry Christmas." Said Edward, his Father.

"Merry Christmas to you too Father." Replied Robert.

" I have a present here for you" Edward said, then passed it to him "here, open it."

What could it be, Robert thought; It was something long and thin. He struggled with the wrapping paper until he got a hold of a loose piece and tugged it, then the paper just came away. He removed the item from the paper and looked at it in awe.

It was a magnificent sabre, handcrafted by his own Father. It was made out of pure silver with a jewelled hilt which was set with four exquisitely cut rubies around the pommel, a highly polished ivory grip, a silver guard plated with the finest gold and the family crest etched on one side of the blade, which was a shield with crossed swords in the middle, a lion on the left standing on it's hind legs and it's front legs outstretched on the shield and on the right of the shield, a lamb on it's hind legs with it's front legs outstretched on the shield. It had with it a leather scabbard adorned with a silver trim around the top and again their family crest etched into the leather.

After standing there admiring the craftsmanship of the weapon, Robert turned to his Father and said. "It is beautiful, Father. Thank you."

"You are welcome, Robert." Replied Edward, then added. "Use it wisely."

"I will have it by my side always." Said Robert.

Robert started swinging the weapon around, trying to get the feel of it, then his Father shouted. "Not in here! Can you do that outside before you break something?"

Robert took his new pride and joy out to the back garden and practised some manoeuvres with his sword. Edward watched him out of the window. He was like a child with a new toy.

After a while, his Mother called him in for dinner so he went back into the house and his Father said to him "you handle that sword well, Robert. It is like you were meant for each other."

"It is perfectly weighted" replied Robert "a magnificent piece of craftsmanship."

"Thank you." Said Edward, looking proud of himself.

"No, thank you Father" Robert replied "it is a wonderful present. More than I could ever wish for."

They sat down to dinner. Robert rested his sword against his chair. It was not leaving his side.

Katherine, Robert's Mother brought the Goose out on a large silver platter, then the Brussels in a dish, then some carrots and finally the gravy, and for dessert, a homemade Christmas pudding with fresh cream. It was a feast fit for a King.

After lunch, Robert and Edward collapsed in their chairs, full to bursting, whilst Katherine made a pot of coffee to wash their dinner down, then in the evening they all sat in the living room for a good talk about Robert's adventures and to relax. He had a lot to tell them. Edward broke out the drinks. Sherry for Katherine, Gin for Robert and Edward.

After a wonderful Christmas, what could better it but spending the new year with his beloved Annabelle.

New years eve approaches and Robert prepares to go to visit Annabelle and her Father to see in the new century. He gathered together some of his best clothes for the party.

"Do you have to go?" said Katherine, a bit upset "can't you invite Annabelle here for the new year?"

"I have to go" replied Robert "there may be some important people there."

Edward took Katherine in his arms and said. "Let him go, Katherine. He has to do what he has to do."

A carriage stopped outside the house for him, Robert stepped up into it and ordered the coachman. "London as fast as you can possibly go."

Edward and Katherine waved him off and he waved back until he was out of sight.

Upon arriving at Admiral Calderdale's house; Robert approached the front door and as he was about to knock, it opened and Annabelle was standing just inside to greet him; she had been looking out for him through the window.

She held her arms wide and wrapped them around Robert's waist so tight that it was stemming his circulation.

"Not so tight" gasped Robert "my sword is digging in me."

"You brought your sword with you?" Asked Annabelle, a bit surprised. Why would he bring his sword with him to a New Years Eve celebration.

"Yes" replied Robert "it was a present from my Father, he made it himself. I wanted to show you it."

They entered the living room and the Admiral was sitting in his armchair in front of the open fire, reading. They sat on a long sofa and the Admiral raised his head away from his book and looked at them.

"Welcome Robert" he said "did you have a good Christmas?"

"Yes thank you Sir." Replied Robert.

"Don't call me Sir when we are at home" the Admiral said "It's John."

Annabelle looked at Robert and asked "are you going to show me your sword now?"

Robert extracted it from its scabbard and pointed the hilt at Annabelle, who took it in her hand. "It's beautiful!" She said. "Your Father is a very talented man."

"Yes and it is all made from silver." Robert replied.

The Admiral turned to Robert from his chair and said. "I am sure you will do it justice. I'm sure it will see plenty of action."

Annabelle escorted Robert to the guest room where he is to sleep while he is there for the new year celebrations.

The morning of New Years eve arrived and Robert awoke, descended down the stairs and he couldn't believe his eyes. The house had been decorated from top to bottom in bunting and balloons; it was like he had woken up in another house.

He entered the living room and looked over to the dining area; there were a lot of tables placed end to end along the walls; all draped with tablecloths ready to accommodate the feast which is to be consumed later.

Robert turned to the Admiral, who was sitting in his favourite chair and asked. "How many people are coming tonight, John?"

The Admiral turned to him and replied. "A lot. There are friends and family coming, as well as important people from the Admiralty. Perhaps you can get to know some of them. It may be useful in the future."

Annabelle entered the room. "Do you want to go for a walk, Robert?" She said.

"That would be nice." Robert replied.

"Be back before 1900 hours!" Shouted the Admiral.

Robert and Annabelle departed the house and went for a long romantic walk by the Thames, hand in hand; they sat on a bench and looked out across the river. Robert had his arm around Annabelle's waist and she rested her head on Robert's shoulder.

They returned to the Admiral's house at 1830 hours. They entered the living/ dining room and all the food and drinks had been laid out. There was enough food for an army.

They started with sandwiches with all kinds of fillings and going anti clockwise around the tables, chicken wings and legs, sausages, rissoles, various salads, all kind of meat; beef, pork and lamb and finishing with desserts, which were apple pies, cherry pies, trifles, fresh fruit.

For drinks they had Brandy, Whiskey, Gin, Rum, Port and Sherry and soft drinks for the children. The Wine and champagne was being left in the cellar until the guests arrive, which will be shortly.

7 O'clock came and the first of the guests started arriving. The Admiral's brother and his wife and son, then two of the Admiral's colleagues arrived together. Before long the room was full.

By nine o'clock everyone had arrived. The Admiral introduced Robert as his future son-in-law to some of his esteemed colleagues in the hope of sometime enhancing his career. Annabelle joined them and stayed by Robert's side all evening.

Everyone was having a wonderful evening. Robert was mingling with as many people as he could. Admiral Calderdale introduced him to some of his most esteemed colleagues at the Admiralty in the hope that it would further his career, since he may one day be his son-in-law.

It was now approaching midnight and a new century. Every person in the room stood looking at the Grandfather clock, waiting.

They all counted down together. "Five-four-three-two-one. Happy New Year!" Then they raised their glasses of champagne and toasted in the New Year and they all started to sing "*should old acquaintance be forgot, and never brought to mind? Should old acquaintance be forgot, and auld lang syne.*"

Robert wrapped both arms around Annabelle, squeezed her tight, whispered in her ear "I love you. Happy New Year" then gave her the biggest kiss ever.

All of a sudden, there was a loud bang and the house shook. One of the guests looked out of the window and shouted "come and look at this!"

Outside, the dark sky was lit up by a multitude of spectacular colours. They were fireworks and what a display, the likes of which some people of that era had never seen before.

Everyone in the house rushed out of the front door and onto the street, which was covered in snow, where people from the nearby houses were already gathered, witnessing the extravaganza.

"It's beautiful!" said Annabelle, then looked into Robert's eyes, who reciprocated and wrapped his arms around Annabelle's waist and squeezed tightly.

People cheered as the rockets rose high into the sky, then erupted into a crescendo of vivid colours, making a variety of noises from bangs to whistles. Some of the guests who had a few too many drinks mimicked the sounds emanating from the skies; with the neighbours staring at them as if they were mad, but if you can't enjoy yourself at a new year celebration, when can you enjoy yourself.

Thirty minutes later, the display subsided and silence ensued so they all sauntered up the steps and back into the house; all, that is, except for Robert and Annabelle, who just stood there in the snow in a romantic embrace. They walked hand-in-hand down to the end of the snow filled road, then back again and into to the house.

They knew that soon Robert will have to go back to sea and they wanted to savour the moment they are having together.

Shortly after, the jollities were over and the guests started dispersing to go home and left Robert, Annabelle and the Admiral on their own in the house, so they decided to retire to bed; the Admiral's staff had left after preparing the feast so that they could see in the new year with their own families and what a feast. They did themselves proud.

Chapter Five

New Century, New Enemy

The day had come when Robert had to go back to sea to continue saving the world from ruthless Pirates. He enjoyed his time off with Annabelle and he was sad to be leaving her, but it has to be done.

He gathered his gear together and walked to the front door followed by Annabelle. They descended down the steps where a coach was waiting to take Robert to his ship at Southampton. He put his bags into the carriage and turned to face Annabelle; she had tears in her eyes, which were running down her face. Robert wiped them away with his finger and said "don't be sad. I will be back before you notice me gone."

"Just make sure you do come back." Annabelle said, with a quiver in her voice.

Robert gave Annabelle one last big kiss, then climbed into the carriage and as it started on its way, he looked back and waved to Annabelle and kept waving until he was out of sight.

Annabelle walked back up the steps and into the house. Her Father was standing there. Seeing she was upset, he put his arms around her and said "don't be too sad dear. He can look after himself and he will be back; of that I am sure."

"I know" said Annabelle "but I didn't know it was going to be this hard."

"You really love him don't you?" Said the Admiral.

"More than anything in the world" replied Annabelle "I don't know what I would do if anything was to happen to him."

Robert arrived at his ship; his crew were waiting on deck to welcome him back on board. Captain Douglas was already there, waiting to set sail.

When everyone was prepared, Captain Douglas gave the order. "Anchors aweigh, full sail heading west!"

Two days into their journey and it was uneventful so far. They passed a school of dolphins elegantly leaping out of the water; following the Dauntless for a little way, as if they were escorting them, then veering off on their own way. The sea was calm and the sky was blue without a hint of any clouds.

Captain Douglas looked over the crew and seeing they were looking a bit bored said. "Cheer up men. You will have enough excitement when we meet up with some Pirates."

Then in low voices they all said in unison. "Aye aye Captain."

Robert turned to Captain Douglas and said "the men are all looking a bit demoralised Captain."

"I know" replied Captain Douglas "but they will see some action very shortly. I am sure of that."

Two more days at sea without any sightings, then, all of a sudden Robert was looking through his spyglass and he saw something in the distance.

"Captain, can you come here?" Robert called.

"What is it Robert?" Enquired Captain Douglas.

"There is a ship in the distance; it looks like an East Indiaman." Said Robert.

"Let me see" said the Captain, taking the spyglass from Robert "it is indeed."

East Indiamen were heavily armed ships, crewed by ruthless merchant seamen, which carried valuable cargo across the Oceans. It takes brave men to try to attack these ships.

They sailed towards it cautiously; as they neared it, it looked as if there was nobody on board.

Captain Douglas called out. "Ahoy there!" But with no reply, he then called again. "Ahoy there on the East Indiaman!"

There was still no answer so he called out again, but louder. "Ahoy there, is there anybody on board?"

"There is something wrong here" said the Captain "it is too quiet. We'll take a boarding party aboard, but be very careful, keep your eyes peeled."

They pulled alongside it as close as they could, then put gangplanks down across the two ships; the Captain took a handful of men, including Robert. When they got aboard the East Indiaman, all they saw were bodies strewn on deck.

"It looks like the work of Pirates." Said Robert, horrified at what he was looking at.

"Indeed." Replied Captain Douglas.

Upon closer inspection, it looked like things were not as they seemed.

Robert looked around the deck at all the bodies "Where's the blood?" He asked, a bit confused.

"What do you mean?" Replied Captain Douglas.

"I mean there are all these bodies but I can't see any blood." Said Robert.

Captain Douglas looked around. "You're right" he said "that's strange."

Robert stooped down to one of the bodies and inspected it closely. "Look at his neck, Captain. What are these marks?"

There were what looked to be two little pin pricks in the side of his neck, like they have never seen before and all of the bodies on deck had the same marks on them.

A lump came to Captain Douglas's throat and he replied "I have no idea, but I have a feeling these are no ordinary Pirates we are looking for."

They went down below and there were more bodies, all with the same marks on their necks. They struggled their way past the bodies, which were blocking the way and down to the hold; none of the cargo had been touched.

"What sort of Pirates are we looking for?" Said Robert, now completely baffled. "All these bodies and no blood, the cargo has not been taken and there is no damage to the ship, which means that they must have been taken by surprise, perhaps a ship posing as a British Naval ship."

"I don't know what we are looking for, but I think we have a serious problem" said the Captain "we will have to leave them here and pick them up on our way back; right now we have to find whoever did this, before we find more scenes like this." Captain Douglas ordered his men back to the Dauntless.

"Full sail ahead" the Captain ordered "heading west."

They set sail towards America; there is a lot of Ocean to cross. Three days had gone by and not a sign of the Pirates, then all of a sudden a shout from the crows nest.

"Land ahoy!"

Captain Douglas looked through his spyglass and sighted an island in the distance "hard to starboard!" He ordered. "Set course for the island. We will see what is there."

When they got close enough to the island without grounding, they dropped anchor and rowed ashore in two boats, then pulled the boats up onto the sand. There were trees all around them. Captain Douglas ordered half of his men to go to the east of the island and he and Robert went to the west.

"Be very wary" said Captain Douglas "we do not know what is on this island."

They set off on their way, hacking through the forest with their machetes, until, eventually they reached a clearing. Ahead of them was a volcano, which had some smoke emanating from it.

They continued to cross the clearing which had dense undergrowth, so it was hard going. As they got half way across, they heard a shot to the east of them.

"That sounds like our men" said Robert "It sounds like they are in trouble."

Captain Douglas turned round and led his men towards where the gunshot came from. When they reached them, it was too late. His men's bodies were strewn around, then he heard a sound, someone groaning. Robert looked around and saw someone moving. It was one of their men, so Robert ran up to him and knelt down beside him.

"Water." Said the man, almost whispering.

Robert took out a flask, opened it and tilted it towards the man's mouth, who then took a sip.

"What happened here?" Asked Robert.

"We were set upon" said the man, his voice was so low that Robert could hardly hear him "they ambushed us. We did not stand a chance."

Robert turned to get to his feet and the man grabbed his arm and pulled him back "there is something else" he said "they had the same marks on their necks as those on the East Indiaman." Then his head fell to one side and he slumped down.

This time a lump came to Robert's throat; he turned to Captain Douglas and said. "He's dead, Captain."

"What did he say?" Asked Captain Douglas.

"He said they were the same men that killed the men on the East Indiaman." Replied Robert.

"How could he be sure?" Asked the Captain.

Robert replied "because they had the same marks on their necks."

"What are we dealing with here?" Asked the Captain, not really expecting an answer.

"We need to get off this island." Said Robert.

"We have to seek out these things first and destroy them. Destroy them all." Said Captain Douglas.

"Very well" said Robert "but we do not know what we are dealing with."

They began to move out, then they heard noises in the trees. The noises seemed to be all around them.

"Draw your swords men" Captain Douglas whispered "be on your guard."

They stood in a circle looking outwards so that nothing can get behind them, then suddenly a yell was heard and a dozen men came out of the woods, charging at them.

Captain Douglas ordered his men to give no quarter and said. "May God go with us on this day."

Just then, there was a loud noise and the earth started shaking. Everyone stopped and looked towards the volcano, which had started spurting out fire and lava from its mouth.

Whilst the volcano was catching everyone's attention, Captain Douglas saw his chance and ordered his men back to their ship and let the volcano do their work for them.

They reached the beach, pursued by the creatures and climbed into their boats, then rowed to the Dauntless and all the creatures could do was watch them sailing away.

As they sailed off, the crew looked back to the island and by now the volcano was in full swing. Molten lava running down the fire mountain and into the forests, completely engulfing the island. Nothing could stand a chance. Piercing screams could be heard coming from the island as the lava swept over the creatures, burning them alive.

"It looks like the Gods were on our side today." Said Robert.

"Indeed." Replied Captain Douglas.

"Do you think they were the men that attacked the East Indiaman?" Robert asked Captain Douglas.

"I think not" replied the Captain "they were natives."

They sailed off into the sunset in search of the Pirate ship.

It was to be another two days before they were to sight anything.

The lookout in the crow's nest shouted down "Ship ahoy!"

There was a ship in the distance; it was a magnificent Galleon, gleaming in the sun, with enormous black sails and it was flying a Jolly Roger, so it seems that they were not afraid of confrontation.

"Can you see what ship it is?" The Captain answered back.

"I have not seen the likes of it before!" Shouted the lookout. "It is a Galleon, but there is something strange about it."

"I can see it" said Robert "it is a Galleon, you had better have a look, it's flying the Jolly Roger. There's something about that ship, but I can't think what it could be."

The Captain took his spyglass out and looked through it at the ship in the distance. "That's no ordinary Galleon." He said

"Can I have another look Captain?" Asked Robert.

The Captain handed him the spyglass.

"I haven't seen anything like it before either; I think we must proceed with caution." Said Robert.

"I agree" said Captain Douglas "let's go in slowly, take the sails down, get the guns manned and ready to fire on my order."

They edged towards the ship; it just sat there in the water, so they edged closer and closer. They pulled alongside; there was no movement on board. There was a name on the bow; it read 'Black Dahlia'.

"Lay the gangplanks men." Ordered the Captain.

They laid the gangplanks down, and then started to cross over to the Black Dahlia, leaving a handful of men on the Dauntless. They boarded the Black Dahlia and couldn't see anybody on board, then a sound was heard from one of the hatches and without warning they were surrounded by hordes of Pirates, brandishing swords.

"Every man for himself" shouted the Captain "watch your backs."

A fight ensued, Robert had his work cut out, fighting three Pirates at once, but he was now highly skilled in the art of swordplay so he can handle himself. He thrust his sword through one of the Pirates, but the Pirate just looked at him and smiled. Robert stared at him open mouthed, not believing what had just happened; then with one movement of the Pirate's hand, he threw Robert against the side of the ship.

Robert looked at him in amazement. "It's not possible" he said to himself "nobody can be that strong and he should be dead."

He rose to his feet and continued fighting, but to no avail. He just could not seem to kill them. Some of the men fired their muskets at the Pirates, but the shots went straight through them.

Meanwhile, on the poop deck; Captain Douglas was in confrontation with the Pirate Captain, they were matching each other blow by blow, then Captain Douglas thrust his sword through the stomach of the Pirate Captain, but he just stood there, looked at him and then put his head around Captain Douglas's neck, sank his teeth in and sucked the life out of him. Captain Douglas fell limp to the floor.

Robert witnessed what was happening on the poop deck and shouted "NO!"

He leapt up onto the poop deck and began to fight the Pirate Captain with anger and hatred in his eyes and the thought of revenge, he got the better of the Pirate and thrust his sword through him and the Pirate Captain just smiled and with one hand, swept Robert aside, down the steps and onto the main deck. Robert then knew that this fight was futile, how can you kill something that will not die.

Now that Captain Douglas was dead, he was next in command and as acting Captain, he had to make an executive decision; he decided to withdraw to fight another day. He needed to find out more about these creatures, because they cannot be human.

"Everyone back to the Dauntless." He ordered.

On the way back to his ship, the Pirate Captain shouted. "The name is Blood, Captain Blood; we will meet again."

"You can be sure of it" Robert shouted back "or my name is not Robert Van Helsing!"

The look on Captain Blood's face then changed, as if he knew that name and he said to himself "yes Mr. Van Helsing, I will look forward to it."

When Robert and his men got back on board the Dauntless, Robert put out the order to fire on the Black Dahlia. All of the guns fired simultaneously, but to no avail; the cannon balls seemed to go right through the ship, whilst not leaving a mark.

"It's impossible!" Said Robert. "How can it be?" Then asked the new second in command "how many dead?"

"Eight, including the Captain" replied the second in command, then added "Captain. I have read about these ships, but I thought they were not real."

"What have you read?" Asked Robert.

"I have read about the ghost ships that sail the oceans, looking for new souls to crew their ships." Replied the second in command.

"I do not believe in such things." Said Robert.

"There are a few things that happened today that cannot be explained." Replied the second in command.

Robert pondered on it for a few moments, then replied "you are right. We must keep our minds open."

"Let's go home and report to the Admiral. We need to find out about these things and their ship" said Robert "they cannot be human."

They set sail on their way home. It will take at least five days of sailing before they get back to England. It was going to be a long and sad journey back home. The Captain was very well liked by his crew. He was a fair man and he treated everybody as equals.

On their way home, they stopped to pick up the East Indiaman to take home so that they could perform tests on them to find out what they are dealing with. Robert put a handful of men on it to sail it back home. They piled all of the bodies into the hold for the journey back.

On the next day; the seas were calm, but something was stirring in the hold of the East Indiaman. The bodies started moving and coming to life. The skeleton crew aboard the ship were unaware that something unusual was occurring down below.

One by one; the dead men slowly walked up the steps, onto the deck and towards the crew. One man spotted them and raised the alarm, then drew his sword and with one swing of his weapon at neck height, he took the head off one of the creatures, who then turned to dust.

"What on God's earth happened to him?" He shouted, dumbfounded.

While he was doing that, another got behind him and placed his head around his neck, opened his mouth to reveal fangs, then sank them into the man's neck, drawing out all of his blood and the man fell to the ground.

The rest of the creatures attacked the remaining crew aboard the ship; they were fighting for their lives, but never stood a chance; there were too many of the creatures.

When the creatures had control of the ship, they went after the Dauntless, which was leading the way.

Robert was unaware of what had just happened on the East Indiaman, until it was nearing them at speed.

"Captain!" Called the lookout. "There is something you must see behind us."

Robert looked through his spyglass. "There is something wrong." He said. "Man the guns."

As the East Indiaman pulled alongside of them; Robert looked over and saw what looked like walking dead, then a blast came from the East Indiaman and ripped a gaping hole in the side of the Dauntless.

Robert ordered to return fire and all of the guns on the port side fired in unison, taking out the side of the East Indiaman; then Robert ordered his gunners to reload and fire again and this time they totally destroyed the East Indiaman. The bow started descending into the briny and the ship began sinking head first, until it completely disappeared, taking everyone and everything on board down with it.

They will have to find another way of discovering what these creatures are. They had lost yet more men to these things.

Five days later they anchored up in Southampton docks, the whole crew were still shell shocked and saddened by the death of their Captain and the other men that lost their lives. Robert and his second in command set off for London to inform the Admiral of what had happened.

They reached London, and then went straight to the Admiralty to see Admiral Calderdale. They went up to his office and knocked on his door.

"Enter!" A voice said.

They entered the room; Admiral Calderdale was sitting at his desk doing some paperwork.

"This is an unexpected pleasure" said the Admiral, looking surprised "hello Robert, where's Captain Douglas?"

"I have some bad news; he is dead. We found an East Indiaman which had been attacked, but it was very strange because all the men seemed to be drained of blood and none of the cargo had been touched, so we went in search of whoever it was that would do this sort of thing and we found them, then we boarded their ship and we were set upon. Unfortunately, Captain Douglas did not make it, but there was something strange about them."

"In what way?" The Admiral enquired.

"We could not kill them. I thrust my sword straight through more than one of them and they never even flinched and they had extraordinary strength" said Robert "including their Captain, who just smiled when I thrust my sword through him. He said his name is Captain Blood."

The Admiral's face turned white as if he had seen a ghost "That's impossible. Captain Blood has been dead for ten years; he was killed when we attacked his ship. I know because I saw it, he was fatally wounded and fell into the sea, nobody could have survived that. Mind you his body was never found, we thought he probably went down to Davy Jones locker; he was the one that gave me this scar" he said, pointing to the scar on his cheek. "Very well, I have to think about this matter. I will check this out. Come to see me tomorrow morning at 10.00 o'clock."

"There is another thing" said Robert "their ship."

"What about their ship?" Replied Admiral Calderdale.

"We put a full salvo of shot into it from our guns and they went straight through it without even leaving a mark on the ship" said Robert, then added "it had a name on it. The Black Dahlia."

A lump came to the throat of the Admiral and he said "that was the name of Captain Blood's ship. Very well I will look into that as well."

"I was going to bring the East Indiaman back so that we could carry out some tests to find out what they are and how to defeat them" said Robert "but they seemed to come alive and attacked our ship, so we had to sink them."

The Admiral looked at them with a puzzled look on his face and said. "Very well. I will see you tomorrow."

Robert and his second in command went to the Black Swan Inn to stay for the night; they had a couple of jugs of ale and something to eat before turning in. It had been a long day.

7.00 o'clock the next morning, Robert awoke with a start, he did not have a good night's sleep, he kept tossing and turning thinking about what happened with the Pirates and Captain Douglas. He woke up his second in command and they went down for some breakfast before going to see the Admiral.

After breakfast they set off to the Admiralty and proceeded to Admiral Calderdale's office and knocked on his door.

"Enter." Came the voice of the Admiral.

They opened the door and entered the room. The Admiral was sitting at his desk again. Annabelle was also there, sitting on the other side of his desk.

"Good morning, Admiral, good morning Annabelle, it's nice to see you." said Robert.

"Father told me what happened to your friend Captain Douglas" said Annabelle "I am so sorry."

"He was a good man, he will be missed." Said Robert, holding back his emotions.

"Alright" said Admiral Calderdale "now we have to get down to business, can you excuse us Annabelle?"

"Certainly Father" said Annabelle, then turned to Robert "will I see you later Robert?"

"I would very much like to" he said "will you be outside in the reception room?"

"Yes." Replied Annabelle.

Annabelle left the room.

Admiral Calderdale turned to Robert; he was looking very serious. "I have been doing some research on what you told me yesterday. What do you know about Vampires?"

"Vampires?" Replied Robert, surprised. "They don't exist."

"Well, everything you told me points to Vampires" said the Admiral "I found out something about their ship as well," he added "it sounds like it was a ghost ship, which is why your guns could not touch it."

Robert turned to his second in command and said "it looks like you were right."

The Admiral then said. "How would you like to take charge of your own ship?"

At twenty one years of age, Robert is due to become the youngest Captain in the Navy.

"Are you offering me a promotion to Captain?" Said Robert, looking surprised.

"I am if you want it" said the Admiral "since Captain Douglas is dead and from what he told me about you, I think you will make a good Captain."

"I would be honoured, Sir." Said Robert.

"Good, I want you to pick a crew that are fearless, because if these are Vampires, they are going to be difficult to kill and we will need people that will kill without hesitation."

"I can start here" said Robert "this is my second in command, a good man and very handy with a sword. His name is James Turner; I would like him to be my First Mate." James Turner was a short stocky man with short black hair and blue eyes.

"Granted, anything else?" Asked the Admiral.

"Yes, if this is going to be as dangerous as you say, we had better find some ruthless seamen. Have you still got Captain Morgan and his Pirates in jail?"

"Yes, they are due to swing on the gallows two weeks from now. Why do you ask?" Replied the Admiral.

"I think it might be an idea to take them with us to fight the Vampires, they have nothing to lose and if they get killed, it will be no loss to us; they are going to die anyway and Captain Morgan does not seem to fear anything."

"You are asking a lot" said the Admiral "I don't know if I can grant this, but I will think about it and discuss it with the board of Admirals. Until then, go and see your Parents for two or three days, because when you go in search of these Vampires you will be gone a long time and I will be honest with you; you may not return."

"Alright. Can I take Annabelle with me to meet my Parents if she wants to go?" Robert asked, in hope.

"Yes, if she agrees. I think I can trust you." Replied the Admiral.

With that, Robert and James exited the Admiral's office. Annabelle was waiting outside in the reception room.

James left the building and left the lovebirds to it and went back to the Black Swan.

"I am going to Southampton to visit my Parents for three days, would you like to come with me?" Asked Robert.

"I would love that but I don't know what my Father will say." Replied Annabelle.

"I have already asked him and he said it was alright as long as you agreed." Said Robert.

"I will have to let him know I am going." Said Annabelle.

"Of course." Said Robert.

They set off for Southampton and arrived there in the afternoon, they arrived at his Parents house.

"What a lovely house." Said Annabelle, pleasantly surprised.

"Yes" replied Robert "my Father made a lot of money in Holland where we came from."

Robert opened the front door and called to his Mother and Father.

"Come here, I want you to meet someone." He shouted.

His Mother appeared from the kitchen.

"Hello" she said, greeting them both "what a nice surprise."

"Hello Mother, this is Annabelle" said Robert "Annabelle, this is my Mother, Katherine."

Katherine took Annabelle's hands in hers and kissed her on both cheeks, which is a traditional welcome in mainland Europe. "It is nice to finally meet you" she said "I have heard a lot about you."

"Where is Father?" Asked Robert.

"In his forge, he is working. I will get him, he will be pleased to see you" said Katherine, then went to the back door, opened it and shouted "Edward, there is someone here to see you."

Edward, Robert's Father appeared at the back door.

"How do you do." He said.

"Hello Father, this is Annabelle" said Robert "Annabelle, this is my Father, Edward."

"Hello" said Annabelle "I am pleased to meet you both."

"Let's go into the lounge and sit down and have a talk, get to know each other better." Said Edward.

They entered the lounge and all sat around a marble coffee table that was positioned in the middle of the room. Katherine made some tea, brought it in and placed it on the table with some home made cakes on a cake stand.

Robert started the conversation. "I have some news to tell you both" he came right out with it "I am now known as Captain Van Helsing."

"You got your promotion!" Said his Father, excitedly. "Congratulations son, I am proud of you."

"So am I." Said his Mother.

"That's the good news. The bad news is that I will not be here long because I have to set sail in three days."

"Where are you going this time?" His Father said.

"We are going after the Pirates that killed Captain Douglas. They are no ordinary Pirates, though." Said Robert.

"What do you mean?" Said his Father.

"The Admiral thinks they are Vampires, but I don't believe in Vampires." Replied Robert.

"What makes him say they are Vampires?" Said Edward.

"After what I told him." Robert replied.

"What did you tell him?" Asked Edward.

Robert explained everything he saw on that fateful day, leaving out nothing. He saw that his Father was looking very interested in what he had to say, but not entirely surprised.

"You don't look surprised at all by what I have told you." Said Robert.

"I am not" he said, then rose to his feet and said "come with me, I want to show you something."

He took Robert into his study. He had a very large bookcase in there; it looked like his very own library. In the centre of the room was a sparkling mahogany writing desk with a leather armchair either side of it. He went to the centre of the bookcase and pulled a book half out and a click was heard and the bookcase seemed to open. It was a door to a secret room.

Before he opened it fully, he turned to Robert and said. "What I am about to show you are relics of my past. I was keeping this from you, I wanted to protect you from it, but now it cannot be helped, it seems it is a family curse."

Robert looked at his Father, curiously.

Edward then opened the door fully and inside was an array of weapons, all forged out of silver, there were stakes, swords, knives, crossbows and the bolts for the crossbows had silver tips. "It may come of a shock to you but I used to be a Vampire hunter before you were born." Edward said.

Robert stood there aghast at what he had seen and heard, his Father had kept it hidden for all these years without him knowing.

"Sit down and I will tell you all I know about Vampires and how it all began." Said Edward, beckoning him to one of the armchairs he had in the study "It all started with Count Vladimir Dracula. He is the original one, he used to be part of the nobility in Transylvania, but it is said that he was cursed by a gypsy he crossed to walk the earth only at night, thirsting only for blood, for eternity. By day he sleeps in his own mausoleum with his private guards protecting him from assassins; now he has created his own army to seek vengeance on this world for making him what he is".

"You said is, so he is still alive." Said Robert.

"Yes, he is still alive, if you can call it alive. Vampires are the walking dead. He is the one that I had been trying to kill for so many years, but he was always one step ahead of me. If you kill him, everyone he has turned and everyone they have turned will turn to dust and it will be the end of Vampires, forever. He comes from Transylvania, but he could be anywhere now." He then added "So tell me about your Captain, how did he die?"

"The Pirate Captain seemed to bite him, and then he just fell to the ground." Said Robert.

"So he was either killed or turned." His Father said. "If he was turned, he will seem to be alive but he will not be your Captain anymore, so if you come up against him, thrust a stake or something silver into his heart. There are only a few things that will kill a Vampire. One is to thrust something, preferably made from silver, into their hearts or cut off their heads. They don't like garlic, but that will just slow them down. Holy water may work if you have enough of it, they don't like sunlight, which will turn them into ash; if you cut them anywhere on their body with anything silver, it will burn them and that should distract them enough for you to finish the job."

"You say they do not like sunlight; but it was daytime when we met them, the sun was shining off their ship." Said Robert.

"Oh, that is bad, it sounds like they have developed immunity to sunlight" replied his Father "that means that nobody will be safe in the daytime either."

Robert was listening to his Father with interest. "I have to go back to London in two days" he said "do you want to come with me and tell Admiral Calderdale what you have told me, and then we can work out a way to kill these things."

"If it will help" said Edward, leading Robert out of the study and back towards the lounge "until then just relax and enjoy yourselves. Annabelle seems like a nice girl."

"She is" said Robert "we love each other. When I get back from hunting these Vampires I am going to ask for her hand in marriage, I will have to ask her Father for permission first, though."

"That's good" said Edward "I wish you luck."

The day came when they had to go back to London to see the Admiral, the three of them, Robert, Annabelle and Edward got in a coach.

"The Admiralty in London, coachman." Ordered Robert.

They sped to London, the coach stopped right outside the Admiralty, they alighted the coach and went inside and up to Admiral Calderdale's office and knocked on the door.

"Enter!" Said the Admiral.

They entered the office. The Admiral was sitting behind his desk again looking over some papers.

"Good morning Admiral," said Robert "this is my Father, Edward. He has something to tell you that you might be interested in; it's about Vampires."

"Ok, I'm listening." Said the Admiral.

Edward then told him everything he had told Robert about Vampires.

Robert then said "He has all the weapons we need to hopefully destroy these creatures."

"That will be useful" said the Admiral, then added "I have here the release papers for Captain Morgan and his men, I have told them that if they were to help then they would be spared the rope, but if they try to escape they will be hunted down like dogs and there will be no mercy, but keep a sharp eye on them and don't turn your backs on them; I still don't trust them."

"You can be sure that we will be very wary, but we need all the help we can get in hunting these Vampires" said

Robert "we must go now and prepare to assemble the crew, but before we go I would like to see Captain Morgan."

"Very well" said the Admiral "you will be escorted down to the dungeons."

Robert proceeded down to the dungeons below the Admiralty and told the jailer to open the door to Captain Morgan's cell. Morgan was sitting on a wooden bed with a straw blanket on top.

"I have here your release papers." Said Robert.

"Is this some kind of a joke?" Replied Captain Morgan.

"No! I am quite serious, but there is one condition" said Robert "you will join me and my crew on a dangerous quest."

"What if I say no?" Asked Captain Morgan.

"Then you will face the gallows" said Robert "I don't know about you, but I will wager the rest of your crew will choose to go with me."

"It looks like I have no choice." Said Captain Morgan.

"You do have a choice" said Robert "certain death or almost certain death."

"That is not much of a choice." Replied Captain Morgan.

"It is the only choice you have." Said Robert.

"Very well." Said Captain Morgan, seeing a way out of the gallows.

"Good" replied Robert, then added "wise choice."

Robert went back to join Annabelle in the Admiral's reception.

Annabelle turned to Robert and said, "Your going to be away a long time aren't you?"

"Yes, I am." Replied Robert.

"I want to go with you!" Demanded Annabelle.

"That's impossible" said Robert "it is too dangerous, and anyway, your Father will never approve."

"I can look after myself" said Annabelle "my Father taught me, I can use a sword as good as many men."

"That maybe so, but you still can't come, these are very dangerous creatures we are going to pursue. They are not human" Robert said "I will never forgive myself if anything happens to you."

"What if my Father says I can go, will you take me then?" Said Annabelle.

"Very well, but I don't think he will allow it." Said Robert, certain that the Admiral will never allow her to go on such a dangerous mission.

Annabelle went to see her Father, she almost begged him to allow her to go with Robert, almost in tears, until her Father could not take any more and agreed to let her go, but to do everything that Robert told her to do and keep out of sight of any trouble. She left the room; Robert was sitting in the reception room.

"My Father has agreed to let me go with you." Said Annabelle.

Robert was very surprised at that decision, but he promised Annabelle he would take her if her Father agreed, so he said. "Very well, if your Father agrees then I will take you, but under protest and at the first sign of any trouble stay out of sight."

"Yes Captain." Replied Annabelle, smiling sarcastically.

They all left the Admiralty. Robert, Edward and Annabelle. Outside, they hailed a coach and set off back to Southampton. A prison coach was taking Captain Morgan and his men straight to the Dauntless.

Robert and company reached Southampton and the Van Helsing household and went inside. James Turner, Robert's first mate met them there, they went to the study, opened the door to Edward's armoury.

James Turner saw the arsenal that Edward had stashed in the secret room and stood there motionless, aghast at what he was seeing. They took out all the weapons they could carry, Edward helped them, then helped them put them in a cart and jumped up onto the cart.

"What do you think you are you doing?" Robert asked his Father.

"I am going with you." Replied Edward.

"No your not!" Said Robert, sternly "it's too dangerous and I will have enough trouble taking care of Annabelle."

"I know Vampires better than anybody" said Edward "I was fighting them before you were born, I can help."

James piped up "I think your Father has a point, Robert."

Robert pondered on it for a while, then said. "Very well; you can come too. You can look after Annabelle if there is any trouble, I just hope I don't live to regret this."

Annabelle stayed at the house with Katherine whilst the men went to load the ship with the vital weaponry needed to dispatch the Vampires, ready for the morning.

They took the weapons to the ship and stowed them away. Captain Morgan and his men were securely locked in the brig. James stayed on board the Dauntless, Robert and Edward went home until the morning. They are due to set sail at dawn.

Chapter Four

The Vampire Hunters

It was 6.00 in the morning on the 25th January in the year 1800. Robert awoke and peered out of the window, it was a dull and misty day, and he woke everyone else up.

"Come on, wake up we must have a hearty breakfast before we set sail." He shouted.

They had their wash, went down to the dining room, Katherine had made them a breakfast that would keep them sated all day, then they got ready to join the crew on the HMS Dauntless.

Katherine started to shed a few tears as they said their goodbyes to her, even her husband is going, but she knows he must go, for he is the only one that really knows about the Vampires and she has friends she can see to keep her company and keep her mind off the horrors that might befall her husband, son and future daughter-in-law.

"Come back safely all of you." She said, tearfully.

"We'll be back, you can count on it" said Robert "I will look after the old man for you." He said, trying to make her smile.

Then they set off for their ship. When they got to the ship, they boarded it, James Turner; the newly appointed First Mate greeted them.

"Good morning Captain." He said.

"Good morning James" replied Robert "where are the Pirates?"

"They are safely locked up in the brig." He said.

"Good, when we are out at sea, let them out, I will want to speak to them. We won't give them arms until we have sight of the Vampires, their ship should be easy to recognise, it will be the one with black sails, the ghost ship."

"Very well" said James "I have prepared your cabin to accommodate Annabelle; there are separate bunks in there."

"Thank you James." Said Robert, then Annabelle and Edward went down below. Edward was sleeping in the next cabin.

They set sail in a westerly direction. When they got about twenty miles away from land, they let Captain Morgan and his men out of the brig and they were summoned on deck. Robert was standing on the poop deck.

"My name is Captain Van Helsing!" He told them "Captain Morgan is no longer a Captain; not on my ship. Here, I am your Captain and you will do well to remember this. If anyone disobeys an order or thinks they are above me then they will be punished according to the law of the sea. Is that clear?"

They all shouted out together "aye aye Captain." Whether they meant it or not is a different matter.

Captain Morgan shouted out "when do we get our weapons?"

"When we sight the Vampire Pirates" replied Robert "and not until then."

Robert then went down below to his cabin; Annabelle was there, she wanted to get changed, but she needed help undoing some buttons on the back of her dress, Robert obliged, then she turned to face him and just then the ship jolted and Annabelle fell into Robert and they fell onto the bunk, Annabelle on top of Robert, they looked into each other's eyes, then their faces got closer and closer until their lips met and they had the most passionate kiss yet, then Robert proceeded to unbutton Annabelle's dress then dropped it to the floor and she did nothing to stop him, then he removed his clothes, tossed them on the floor and they both lay on the bed, their naked bodies in a love embrace as they proceeded to make love, the swaying of the ship in the ocean making it more intense, their bodies gleaming from the sun shining through the porthole. They had confirmed their love for each other.

"You are the first person I have ever given myself to." Said Annabelle.

"You are my first also." Replied Robert.

They got dressed and went up on deck together. When Annabelle appeared on deck, there were whistles and lewd remarks aimed at her from the Pirates, which infuriated Robert.

"Enough of that!" Raged Robert. "If I hear one more remark, those responsible will feel the sting of the cat." Then there was deadly silence.

They carried on westward on their quest. On the second day of their voyage, the lookout in the crow's nest shouted "LAND AHOY!"

Robert took out his spyglass and spotted an island in the distance and decided to investigate it.

He turned to James and said "we will drop anchor about a mile off shore and take a dozen men to investigate the island; you will stay here in case anything goes wrong and train the guns on the island in case we need them."

"Aye aye Captain." Said James.

"Father, you come with us." Said Robert.

They gathered as many weapons as they could comfortably carry. Robert had his sword in the scabbard and a couple of silver stakes tucked into his belt. Edward picked up his crossbow and the silver tipped bolts to go with it which he kept in a quiver, and the rest of the men gathered swords and knives. They also took some muskets in case they had to deal with natives.

They lowered their boat into the water, then climbed down the ropes into it and rowed towards the island. It looked deserted as they approached it, they grounded the boat on the sand and they all jumped out onto the sand. Just beyond the sand there were large hills with trees and shrubbery growing up them, to the left and right of them were trees, they were like forests.

"Ok, Father, I will take half the men and go to the right and you take the other half and go to the left, if you find anything fire your musket." Ordered Robert.

They set off through the thicket; Robert going one way and Edward, the other. They were having to use their cutlasses to clear a path through. A few minutes in, they came across a waterfall cascading into a pool, it looked like a paradise, then suddenly Robert heard a gunshot so they rushed to where the shot came from, they met up with Robert's Father and the others.

"What's wrong?" Said Robert to his Father.

"Look over there." Edward replied, pointing.

Robert looked to where his Father was pointing and he saw a mound of bodies, which looked like natives. On closer inspection, he saw that they had the same marks on their necks as the crew of the East Indiaman and they were all drained of blood. It looked like the remains of a Vampire dinner party.

"It looks like they were here" said Robert "we are going the right way."

"We had better burn these bodies in case they turn." Said Edward.

"Very well" agreed Robert "make it quick, we have to get going."

They set alight to the bodies and when they were well alight, they went on their way back to the ship. Walking through the forest, they heard some noises coming from behind the trees.

"What was that?" Said Robert.

"I don't know." Replied Edward.

"Be on your guard!" Ordered Robert.

All of a sudden out of nowhere came a dozen Vampires. So quick that some of the men never had a chance. The rest of the men drew their weapons and started fighting off the Vampires. Robert and Edward stood back to back to protect each other.

Edward drew one of the bolts from the quiver, loaded it into his crossbow and let it fly. It pierced one of the Vampires straight through the heart, then it just disintegrated into dust.

Robert drew his sword and started to fight another of the Vampires. His sword was clattering against the Vampire's then they locked their swords and Robert saw his chance: he drew one of the stakes from his belt and thrust it straight into the heart of the Vampire and it turned to dust, then another one ran towards him and Robert swung his sword at the Vampire and took its head clean off.

After they dispatched all of the Vampires; they looked around them at the dead. They had lost a few men, but that is to be expected in this fight against evil. They built a pyre and placed all the dead on top, then set it alight. They had to burn them in case they turned. After it was well alight, they carried on their way.

They reached the beach, jumped in their boat and rowed back to the Dauntless; they climbed aboard and set sail.

"What happened on that island?" Asked James.

"The Vampires were there" replied Robert "there were bodies; a lot of bodies and they left some Vampires waiting there for us. They know we are on their trail."

"This is like when I was after Dracula" said Edward "he always seemed to be one step ahead of me. It is like they can read your mind."

It was starting to get dark so they dropped anchor for the night. They positioned the lookouts around the sides of the ship. It was a peaceful, clear night with the stars shining bright in the sky and the brightness of the moon shimmering across the ocean.

Morning came and everyone arose to a cold day, although the sun was beating down, there was quite a chill in the air.

They had their sails up, there was quite a breeze so they could make some headway. Robert was standing on the bow of the ship looking out over the vast ocean, Annabelle came to join him.

"You look a bit upset" she said "what happened on that island yesterday?"

"It was awful. There were more bodies, lots of them" said Robert "we have to stop these before they kill any more people."

Just then a voice came from the crow's nest "SHIP AHOY!"

"Is it them?" Asked Robert.

"No, it looks like a Clipper." Said the lookout.

Robert looked through his spyglass, it was indeed a Clipper. They headed towards it, taking it slow. A lump came to Robert's throat, not knowing what horrors they are going to find on that ship. They approached it with caution. Yet again, there seemed to be nobody on board.

"Pull alongside her" ordered Robert "put the gangplanks down, give Mister Morgan and his men some weapons just in case we need them." He looked at Captain Morgan. "You and your men are coming with me to do the job you escaped the rope for."

"I would like to go with you." Said Edward.

"Very well Father" said Robert "but keep close to me."

They walked across the gangplanks cautiously, then went onto the deck of the Clipper. There was no sign of anybody on the deck. Robert and Edward went to the steps leading down to the cabins, while the rest of the men remained on deck, Robert opened the door. There were bodies strewn down the steps, they brushed slowly and carefully past the bodies and into the Captain's quarters. The Captain was slumped over his table.

"Oh my God!" Said Robert, horrified "How many more people are going to get killed before we catch these creatures?"

They turned to walk out, Robert was in front, they started to go back up the steps to the deck, they got half way up and Edward felt something grab his leg, he looked down and saw one of the crewmen of the Clipper, his face was white and when he opened his mouth, Edward saw that he had fangs.

"Robert!" He shouted. "They've turned."

"What do you mean?" Replied Robert.

"The Vampires have turned them, they are now Vampires, we must destroy them, all of them. You had better tell the rest." Said Edward.

Then Edward spun round with his sword in his hand and with one swoop took off the Vampires head and it turned to dust in front of him, then they all seemed to come alive, including the Captain. Edward headed up the stairs to the deck to join Robert. Captain Morgan and his Pirates were fighting the Vampires on deck, who seemed to appear from every orifice of the ship, so Robert and Edward helped them out. The Vampires seemed to come from nowhere, but they had to get them all and make sure none of them escape.

Edward was crossing swords with one of the Vampires then he got his chance, he thrust his sword straight through the Vampire's heart and it turned to dust, then he heard a sound behind him, he spun round and a Vampire turned to dust in front of him and Captain Morgan was standing there with his sword held aloft. He had saved Edward's life.

"Thank you." Said Edward.

"Don't mention it" said Captain Morgan "but I'm not going to make a habit of it."

"How many more of them are there?" Said Captain Morgan, turning to Robert.

"I don't know" replied Robert "the more we kill, the more there seem to be, but we must be sure there are no Vampires left alive on this ship."

After they finished with the Vampires on deck, they went down below to make sure there were no more anywhere on the ship. When they were sure, Robert ordered everyone back to the Dauntless. When they got back on board the Dauntless, Robert assessed the casualties.

"How many men have we lost?" Asked Robert.

"I've lost three men." Said Captain Morgan.

"And we have lost four." Said Edward.

Robert ordered some shots from their guns into the Clipper to sink it. The Clipper started to sink, it seemed to go down in slow motion at first, then the bow came up and it suddenly disappeared, on its way to the bottom of the Ocean. When it had completely gone they set sail to carry on their quest for Captain Blood and his Vampire Pirates. They had by now covered a lot of the Atlantic Ocean; they had been at sea for ten days and seen the damage the Vampires have caused which reminded them why they are on this mission.

Robert went down to his cabin where Annabelle was waiting; she couldn't bear to be on deck while Robert was on the other ship fighting Vampires. He had an injury on his arm, a cut from a sword.

"You've been hurt!" Said Annabelle, looking worried.

"It's only a flesh wound." Replied Robert, then he asked Annabelle to bandage it up for him, which she did.

Edward came down to Robert's cabin.

"You fought well out there son, I am proud of you." He said.

"Thank you Father, but it is my job, if I can't do it then I can't expect my men to do it." Said Robert.

Night was falling, it had been a long day again and everyone was tired. Robert ordered six men to stand lookout while they went to catch up on some sleep. It was a clear night, the stars were shining in the sky, nothing was stirring, it was going to be an easy night for the lookouts.

Dawn broke, the sun was rising in the sky, it looks like it is going to be a nice day. The deck was starting to stir with the crew. Robert awoke, Annabelle was already awake, they had a wash then went to the galley to have breakfast. After breakfast they went up on deck. Captain Morgan was on the poop deck looking out to sea; Robert went up to join him and stood next to him.

"You fought well yesterday, Morgan." He said.

"I have fought worse things." Morgan replied, vainly.

"Thank you for saving my Father's life." Said Robert.

"Well, we need all the men we have got" Morgan replied "anyway, he knows more about these Vampires than anyone else on this ship, so he is our best chance of finding and defeating them."

It is a calm day and there is no sight of anything, just clear skies and calm sea with the horizon ahead of them. Maybe they can have an easy day so that they are refreshed for when they catch up with Captain Blood. Edward and

Annabelle joined them on deck, making the most of the peace and quiet.

"Hello Annabelle, hello Father." Said Robert.

"Hello Robert." They both replied.

"Is there any sign of the Vampires yet?" Asked Annabelle.

"No, not yet" replied Robert "but we can't be too far from them."

It was indeed a quiet day. The evening drew in; the sun was setting on the horizon. Robert decided to stand guard that night and he picked another five men to stand guard with him. Annabelle stayed on deck with him and they just talked to each other all night in each other's arms, watching the sun go down and the moon rising in the sky.

"What will you do when you finally defeat these Vampires?" Annabelle asked Robert.

"I don't know" replied Robert "they will probably send me on another mission. There is a lot of evil in this world."

"I hope you find them soon." Said Annabelle.

Dawn was breaking on the fifth day of their voyage, it looks like it is going to be another nice day, and the sun was beating down on the deck of the Dauntless. There was a bit of a wind to carry them along.

Robert and Annabelle went down below to Robert's quarters for some sleep, Robert told James turner, the First Mate to wake them if anything happens. They got to his quarters and jumped in their own bunks, they were so tired that they went off as soon as their heads hit their bunks.

Noon came and Robert awoke, Annabelle was already awake. She was sitting there staring at him.

"What's wrong Annabelle?" Asked Robert.

"Nothing" replied Annabelle "I am just thinking."

"What are you thinking about?" Robert asked.

"I am thinking how much I am in love with you." Replied Annabelle.

Robert went over to her on her bunk and put his arm around her, pulled her closer to him then he started to kiss her on her neck then on her cheek then on her lips and she reciprocated. They were in an embrace, Robert felt some buttons on the back of her dress and proceeded to unbutton them one by one until they were all undone, then he pulled the back apart and pulled her dress down over her legs then her feet until it was clear and tossed it onto his bunk, then he proceeded to remove her corset then the rest of her underwear, after that he removed his clothes bit by bit.

When they were both as nature intended he laid her gently on her bunk and started to caress her breasts then worked his way down, Annabelle shivered in anticipation as he kissed her all over.

After the foreplay he got on top of her and made such passionate love that neither of them had ever felt before, even better than the last time. After they finished they kissed again, got dressed and went up on deck. James Turner was standing at the bow with Edward, looking across the Ocean. Robert and Annabelle joined them.

"It looks like there are dark clouds ahead" said Robert "we had better prepare for another storm. All hands on deck!" He cried. "Annabelle, go to your quarters and stay there."

"Aye aye Captain." Said Annabelle, as she shuffled down the steps to the cabin.

The storm came on them quickly; it was a fierce one with waves fifty feet high. The Dauntless was getting a battering. The ship was rocking from side to side, at times feeling like it is going to capsize. One of the men was by the side and a gigantic wave appeared and swept him off the deck and out to sea. They lost a few men in that storm, which was something they did not need when they have to come up against Vampires.

The storm subsided and it became clear again, there was a lot of damage done to the Dauntless and a lot of repairs to be done, which could not be done at sea.

"We have to find some land to repair our ship." Robert said to James.

"I will have a look at the charts and see if there is any land nearby." Said James.

James disappeared down below. He was gone about thirty minutes, then he reappeared on deck, he went up to the helm where Robert was waiting alongside Edward and Annabelle, carrying a chart.

"There is an island not far from here" he said, pointing to a position on the chart "it looks like quite a large island; it should be good for us to drop anchor for repairs and maybe for supplies. We are getting a bit short."

They headed in the direction of the island; it was getting a bit dark now, going into the evening.

"We will drop anchor here for the night" said Robert "we will go to the island in the morning; I don't want to risk grounding us on the rocks."

It was a calm night; the moon was shining bright in the sky. Robert and Annabelle were standing on deck looking up at the stars. Robert had his arm around Annabelle's waist and she was resting her head on his shoulder.

"What are you going to do when you catch up with the Vampires?" Asked Annabelle.

"We will have to destroy them all" Robert answered "if we miss any of them then it could all start again in the future."

"Be careful" said Annabelle "I don't want to lose you. I don't know what I would do without you."

"I'll be careful, don't worry" said Robert "I owe Captain Blood for what he did to Captain Douglas."

James came up on deck and joined Robert and Annabelle.

"It seems like it's going to be a quiet night" he said "you two can go down below and rest; I will stand on watch tonight."

"Very well, we will see you in the morning." Said Robert.

They went below to their quarters; they were both tired so went straight to bed. Robert had a restless night. He was having nightmares about what he had seen; the carnage the Vampires had caused, the faces of his men being slaughtered.

Dawn broke, it is raining. Robert awoke, sweating; then Annabelle arose and looked over to Robert. "What's wrong?" She asked.

"I had nightmares last night, terrible nightmares." Robert replied.

"What sort of nightmares?" Asked Annabelle.

"About the Vampires." Said Robert.

Annabelle went over and sat next to Robert on his bed, put her arm around him and comforted him. "It's alright, I am here" she said "let's have something to eat, you may feel better afterwards."

They had breakfast then went up on deck. James was standing on the bow looking out through his spyglass.

"Good morning" said James to Robert and Annabelle "I can see an island on the horizon; I think it is maybe one hour away."

"Good" said Robert "weigh anchor, set sail for the island."

As they neared the island James was searching through his spyglass for a good place to drop anchor. He spotted a sheltered bay, so they headed there and dropped anchor.

"We will take two boats with us" said Robert "James, you stay here and guard the ship. Father, you come with us. We will find out how friendly the natives are first, we had better take some weapons just in case these are savages, or worse."

"Can I come?" Asked Annabelle.

"No" said Robert, assertively "it's too dangerous, until we find out what is on the island. You stay here and wait for us, we shouldn't be too long."

They climbed into the boats and the crew that were staying on the Dauntless lowered them down into the water. They rowed towards the island; Robert was looking through his spyglass. There was a beach which was deserted and beyond the beach there was a majestic forest with dense growth, and hills in the background. They reached the shallow water; two men from each boat jumped out into the water and pulled the boats onto the beach.

"We'll go this way." Ordered Robert, pointing to the right.

They set on their way into the forest, using their cutlasses to make a path through the trees, it was hard going. They eventually came to a clearing, they could see in the distance a volcano which looked inactive, to the left was a waterfall which cascaded into a pool. They continued walking straight on, then they heard noises; they were voices, people talking.

"Take cover men" Robert whispered "in those trees." He pointed to the trees on the right.

They took cover and watched as half a dozen natives came out of the forest to their left, brandishing spears. Two of them were carrying a pole on each of their shoulders and hanging from the poles was a large boar, which had been slaughtered for food.

Robert and his men decided to follow the natives to find out where their village is. They followed them as they walked past the pool and waterfall and into the forest the other side of it.

A little time later, they came to the edge of the forest; the village was just beyond that, across a plain and down a hill. The natives walked down into their village. Robert told his men to stay back, whilst he and his Father crawled through the undergrowth to where it started to descend down to the village.

Robert took out his spyglass and looked through it. He could see that it was quite a large village, with lines of mud huts, with smoke exuding from the chimneys. He passed the spyglass to his Father, who then looked through it.

"What do you think, Father?" Asked Robert.

"I don't know" replied Edward "they don't look like savages."

Just then, Robert felt something sharp digging in his back, he turned his head slowly and saw some natives behind them with spears pointing at them, then the rest of his men appeared from the forest with more natives holding spears on them. The natives beckoned to them to get to their feet, which they did, slowly, then the natives led them down to the village at the end of their spears.

They reached the edge of the village, and then continued into the village; as they walked through, people came out of their huts and watched as they carried on walking down the middle of the road.

At the end of the road was a house, which was different than the rest of the buildings. It was built with wood. It was built on stilts with steps leading up to the door and a veranda, which encircled the house.

The natives led them to this house and then one of them walked up the steps and entered the house. He appeared a few minutes later with another man, this was a white man in his sixties, he was of slim build with short white hair, and he was carrying a cane to assist with his walking for he had a limp on his right leg.

"Greetings, the name is Caruthers, Dr. George Caruthers" he said "and who might you be?"

Robert stepped forward and said "My name is Captain Robert Van Helsing of His Majesty's Navy, this is my Father, Edward and these are my men from the HMS Dauntless. Are you in charge here?"

"Yes" answered Dr. Caruthers "come inside where we can talk."

Dr. Caruthers led them into his house through the front door. Robert and Edward followed him in. Robert ordered the rest of the men to wait for them outside.

It was a basic house; there was a table in the centre of the living room surrounded by four chairs. Ahead, a door led to the bedroom with a crude wooden bed and a straw mattress, to the left of the bed was a bathtub carved out of a tree trunk.

Dr. Caruthers invited them to sit around the table.

"Would you like some tea?" Asked Dr. Caruthers.

"That would be nice" replied Robert, then added "I must say it makes a good change to see a friendly face on our travels."

Dr. Caruthers called one of the natives and asked him to make a pot of tea for them all.

"What brings you to my island?" Enquired Dr. Caruthers.

"We ran into a storm last night and we suffered quite a lot of damage to our ship" replied Robert "we thought we might find the materials here to repair it."

"What are you looking for?" Asked Dr. Caruthers.

"Wood for the masts and also for the deck." Replied Robert.

"We have plenty of wood here" said Dr. Caruthers "you are welcome to take as much as you like, we have some men here that will help you repair your ship too if you would like. Anything for His Majesty's Navy."

"That's very kind of you" said Edward "that will be appreciated."

"So how did you end up here?" Robert asked Dr. Caruthers.

"I was shipwrecked a long time ago with a few other crew members. I don't know how long, I have lost all concept of time on this island" said Dr. Caruthers "I was the Doctor on a tea clipper, we were trading tea when we ran aground on the other side of the island. I don't remember much, I must have passed out. I opened my eyes and we were on the beach, there were natives all around just staring at us, digging us with their spears; I suppose they were curious. They had probably not seen anything like us before, then they brought us here to their village and treated us as they did their own. We taught them things like how to build houses from wood. We taught them how to speak English among other things and they eventually made me the head of their village."

"Where are the rest of your crewmen?" Asked Robert.

"The rest of the crew were picked up by a ship about a year later, I remember it because it was a strange ship. I have never seen the like before, it had black sails. I decided to stay here; I thought I could help these people evolve. Back home I would be just another person; here I feel important."

"It will be dark soon; you must stay as our guests for the night." He added.

"Thank you for the offer" said Robert "but we must get back to our ship, we will return in the morning. The ship that picked up your crew, you said it had black sails. Did you see any name on it?"

"Yes, there was a name on the bow" said Dr. Caruthers "I think it was" he thought for a minute "Black something."

"Black Dahlia?" Prompted Robert.

"Yes that's it!" Shouted Dr. Caruthers "The Black Dahlia."

Robert looked at Edward, Edward looked at Robert, then they both looked at Dr. Caruthers and Robert said. "That's the ship we are on the trail of, they are Vampires."

"VAMPIRES!" Shouted Dr. Caruthers, startled. "Do they exist? I have heard of them, but I thought they were just a myth."

"No" said Edward "they are very real, we have come across them, they are virtually immortal and very powerful." They told Dr. Caruthers all about Vampires.

It was time to get back to their ship. They made their way through the village and out towards the forest, then through the forest to the beach, into their boat and back to the Dauntless.

Back on board the Dauntless, Annabelle was waiting on deck with James.

"You were gone a long time, we were getting worried about you, we were going to send a search party to look for you" said James "what did you find?"

"They are friendly natives" said Robert "the head of their village is an English Doctor; they are going to help us with our repairs in the morning."

"Are you sure you can trust them?" Asked James, a bit wary of them.

"Quite sure" replied Robert, then added "anyway, we have no choice."

Night was drawing in; it was time to retire for the night. Robert and Annabelle went down below to their cabin;

everyone else went to their own quarters leaving half a dozen men to stand guard for the night.

The next morning, Robert got up early, had something to eat then went up on deck, Captain Morgan was on the poop deck, looking out to sea, and Robert joined him. "What are you looking for?" He said.

"Just thinking" said Captain Morgan "I was thinking how I got here. What's going to happen to me after we have destroyed the Vampires?"

"I don't know, that will be up to the authorities" said Robert "I will see what I can do for you, but you will have to come back with me to answer for your crimes, maybe I can get your sentence reduced to time in gaol."

Robert then added. "So how did you get into this position?"

"It all started when I was young" started Captain Morgan "my Father was abusive to my Mother and myself. He sent me to a workhouse so that I can make some money for his drinking obsession, until one day I arrived home late; he went for me, but my Mother stepped in front of him and he pushed her onto the fireplace and killed her. I was then filled with rage; I picked up the first thing I saw and hit my Father over the head with it and then he too was dead. Two soldiers saw me with the weapon in my hand, so I had to run."

"Why didn't you stay and tell them what really happened?" Robert asked.

"I was afraid they would not believe me and send me to the gallows. I was too young to die." Replied Captain Morgan.

"How did you become a Pirate?" Asked Robert.

"I smuggled aboard a ship in the docks" Captain Morgan replied "but I did not know that it was a Pirate ship until it was too late. It was the Audacious."

"That is a sad story" said Robert "when we get home; if we get home, we will tell that story to the courts and maybe they will show leniency."

"Why would you do this for me?" Asked Captain Morgan.

"Because I believe in giving people another chance and I think you can change" replied Robert, then added "and you have so far been invaluable to me."

Robert assembled his crew to choose some men to go to the island. They rowed to the island went through the forest and down to the village. Dr. Caruthers was waiting there for them; he got some of the natives to carry the wood they needed to the ship. He asked Robert and Edward to stay so that he could have a word with them.

"I didn't sleep last night" he said "I was thinking about what you said about Vampires. If the Vampires can turn humans into them, can it work the other way round? I would like to try to find a cure."

"Do you think you would be able to do that?" Asked Robert, sounding almost sceptical.

"I can try" replied Dr. Caruthers "I am a scientist as well as a doctor, but they would not let me practise back home; they called me the mad doctor; that is why I ended up on a clipper. It was the only job I could get. It will be nice to do some good and prove them all wrong. I will need some equipment, though."

"Very well" said Robert "make a list and I will do my best to get you all that you need. If it works I will make sure everyone in England knows what you have done for humanity."

"Thank you." Said Dr. Caruthers.

Dr. Caruthers had already made his list, which read: - microscope, syringes, acid, alkaline solution, test tubes, various chemicals and Vampire's blood.

Robert read down the list. "Vampire's blood!" He exclaimed.

"Yes" said Dr. Caruthers "I will need Vampire's blood to test and maybe mix with other elements."

"Very well" said Robert "I will do my best, but it will not be easy. Vampires are normally the ones that take the blood from humans."

They finished repairing the ship, it took them four hours and it looked as good as new. They thanked Dr. Caruthers then departed; but before departing they marked the island on the map so that they could easily locate it when they return.

They set sail again on their quest for Captain Blood and his band of Vampires; the storm the other night had set them back. They had their full sails up and there was quite a strong wind so they can make up some ground.

Two more days at sea had gone by, then they had a stroke of luck. There was the shout they had been waiting for. "SHIP AHOY" from the crows nest. Robert took out his spyglass, he saw the Black Dahlia in the distance.

"That's them" he said to James "full sail ahead, break out the weapons. Let's finish this, then we can go home."

The Vampires must have seen them because they turned and were going away from them, it seemed like they were running away, but the Dauntless was too fast for the Dahlia, they were closing in on them.

They got broadside of the Dahlia, then swung over on ropes, Robert first, followed by James then Captain Morgan and Edward then the rest of the crew followed. Edward fired a bolt from his crossbow up to the crows nest. The lookout tipped over the edge and started falling, half way down he disintegrated, raining ash on the deck. Robert fought his way through to the helm, he saw a man standing there with his back towards him, the man felt his presence and turned round.

"Captain Douglas!" Cried Robert. "You're alive."

"Hello Robert" said Captain Douglas "it is nice to see you again."

"I thought you were dead" said Robert "I saw you laying there lifeless."

"Yes I was" said Captain Douglas "but Captain Blood brought me back to life and made me immortal. I can do the same for you and we can fight side by side again like the old times."

"I don't want to be immortal" said Robert "it is not natural."

Edward was on the main deck; he heard the commotion on the poop deck and looked up. He saw Robert with Captain Douglas.

"Robert, NO!" He cried.

Robert turned round to his look at his Father; as he was looking away, Captain Douglas opened his mouth to reveal his fangs and moved closer to Robert's neck, just then Robert turned round and reeled back in shock as he saw Captain Douglas's fangs, Edward let a bolt fly from his crossbow.

Captain Douglas turned his head towards Edward, reached his hand out and caught the bolt, then he smiled and looked down at the bolt; then before he could take a second breath, Edward loaded his crossbow and let another bolt fly. This one flew straight and true into the heart of Captain Douglas, whose face then became distorted in agony, it looked like he was ageing a hundred years every second then he turned into a pile of ash at Robert's feet. Robert just stood there, frozen on the spot. It was then that Robert realised how evil these creatures really are.

They dispatched all the Vampires they could see, except one, which they needed for Dr. Caruthers to develop his serum. They tethered him with chains and shackles and put him in the brig. There was no sign of Captain Blood on the Dahlia. They searched for him inside and out, but to no avail, was this a decoy ship to throw them off the scent? They had lost a few good men in the battle.

After searching the Dahlia, they went back to the Dauntless and before they departed on their way, they fired some shots into the hull of the Dahlia and watched it sink to the bottom of the Ocean. It seems that this ship was not a ghost ship like the genuine Black Dahlia.

They tethered the Vampire securely in chains ensuring that there is no way he could escape them, then locked him in the brig.

Robert went down below to his cabin. Annabelle was sitting there on a bench. Seeing Robert was a bit upset, she asked "what's wrong, Robert?"

Robert replied "It was Captain Douglas."

"What do you mean?" Asked Annabelle.

"Captain Douglas was the Captain on that ship" Robert said "but it wasn't the Captain Douglas I knew. It was a Vampire."

"What did you do to him?" Annabelle asked.

"My Father killed him" said Robert "Captain Douglas tried to make me into a Vampire, so my Father killed him."

Annabelle put her arm around Robert and pulled him towards her and said "I am so sorry, Robert."

"I think it was for the best" said Robert "now he is free."

Seven days later they sailed into Southampton docks; they were glad to see the shores of England again. After they had docked, Robert, Annabelle and Edward went to Edward's house for the night. Katherine was happy to see them all again. This time shedding tears of joy.

"You must all be ravenous." Said Katherine.

"I could eat the hind leg off a donkey." Replied Edward, jovially. He was just happy to be home again with his lovely wife.

They all sat around the dining table and Katherine made them all a sumptuous meal and Edward brought a couple of bottles of wine from his cellar. After dinner they all retired to the living room and sat talking about their exploits; except Robert, who was just sitting there with a glass of wine in his hand, staring into space. He was thinking about what happened to Captain Douglas. The sight he had seen would haunt him for the rest of his life.

Edward knew what Robert was thinking about, which was only natural because Captain Douglas had been his friend as well as his Captain. He tried to comfort him and said "I am sorry about Captain Douglas, but it was either you or him. I had to make a split decision."

"I know" said Robert "it was not your fault. You saved my life and it was for the best for Captain Douglas. I will get over it, but I want Captain Blood for myself. He will pay dearly for what he has done."

The next morning it was time to report back to Admiral Calderdale. Robert and Annabelle took a coach to London and the Admiralty. They went up to the Admiral's office. The Admiral was pleased to see them.

"What have you got to report?" Said the Admiral. "Did you find Captain Blood and his crew?"

"Yes and no" replied Robert "we found the Black Dahlia and we destroyed the crew, but Captain Blood was nowhere to be found, it seems it was a decoy and not the real Black Dahlia. The Captain was an old friend of ours; Captain Douglas, but he was a Vampire. Captain Blood had turned him."

"Where is Captain Douglas now?" Asked Admiral Calderdale.

"He is dead" replied Robert, looking saddened "he tried to turn me, but my Father shot him with his crossbow."

"Are you sure he is dead?" Asked the Admiral "I thought Captain Blood was dead all those years ago, but he was still alive."

"Yes" replied Robert "I saw him turn into a pile of dust at my feet."

"Very well" said the Admiral, a bit disappointed "but you will have to go back out there, he will have to be stopped, but in the meantime you must stay with us for a few days."

"We have made a significant discovery, though" said Robert "we have found a doctor who thinks he can make a cure to turn the Vampires back into humans."

"Really!" Said the Admiral, taken aback. "That would be a breakthrough if it works, what do you think his chances are."

"He seems fairly confident" said Robert "but he needs some equipment for his research. We have captured a Vampire for him to work on; here is a list of what we need."

"Very well, I will see what I can do, let us hope it works" said the Admiral "if that's all, Annabelle will take you home and make you comfortable, I will be home in about two hours after I have finished my work here."

Robert and Annabelle took a coach back to the Admiral's house, freshened up and awaited the arrival of the Admiral.

On his arrival, the cook prepared a sumptuous feast for them all and the Admiral went down to his cellar and selected a couple of bottles of his special wine to have with dinner.

After dinner Annabelle was tired so she retired to bed, it was nice to sleep in a comfortable bed after all that time at sea. Robert stayed up to talk to Admiral Calderdale, who lit up a cigar. He offered one to Robert, who declined on the fact that he does not smoke. They got on well with each other, then Robert got up the nerve to ask the Admiral.

"Annabelle and I are in love" he said, then hesitantly added "I would like to ask you for her hand in marriage."

The Admiral sat back in his chair not entirely surprised, then took a long puff on his cigar and there was silence for a few moments; then the Admiral spoke.

"What does Annabelle think about it?" He asked.

"I haven't asked her yet" Robert replied "I wanted to seek your approval first."

"I admire that" said the Admiral, giving a little smile "you have my approval, if Annabelle says yes. I only want her to be happy. I would be proud to have you as a son-in-law and I think you will make Annabelle very happy. If you do not you will have me to deal with."

"Thank you Admiral, I will do my best. I will propose to her tomorrow." Said Robert, gleaming.

"Very well, but if you are going to be my son-in-law, don't call me Admiral at home; Call me John or Father." He ordered, and then they both retired late after having a good man to man chat.

Dawn came; the sun was rising in the sky. Robert awoke and smelt breakfast cooking. He freshened up in the bathroom, and then went downstairs, he was the last one up; Annabelle and her Father were sitting at the table in the dining room drinking tea whilst waiting for Robert before starting breakfast.

After breakfast, Robert asked Annabelle if she would go for a walk with him, she agreed. They went for a walk and ended up in Hyde Park where they went the first time they went out together, they also sat on the same bench, so that it was more romantic.

Robert turned to Annabelle, took her right hand, looked straight into her beautiful eyes and said hopefully "I love you Annabelle, I want to spend the rest of my life with you. Will you do me the honour of giving me your hand in marriage?"

Annabelle looked at him stunned, she was speechless at that moment, and then she said "I have dreamt of this since I met you, but can you ask my Father for his approval? It will mean a lot to me. Apart from you, he is the only thing I have."

"I have, and he was delighted." Said Robert.

Annabelle smiled and opened her arms, put them around Robert and squeezed tight, tears of joy exuding from her eyes, she was so happy her dream is becoming a reality. They sat there in a tight embrace for what seemed an eternity.

The next step is to agree a date for the wedding. It has to be an early one because Robert will have to go to sea again soon. They walked back home to the Admiral's house to arrange the day with the Admiral. Robert will also have to let his Parents know.

They agreed that it should take place on Friday the next week, they will get married in Saint Paul's church in London, so now Robert has to travel back to Southampton to inform his Parents.

They were happy for him and said that they will travel up on the Friday morning for the wedding. Robert will have to stay with them on the Thursday night and travel to London with them on Friday morning. James Turner was to be Robert's best man and the rest of the crew from the HMS Dauntless were also invited.

The preparation for the wedding begins. Admiral Calderdale took his late wife's wedding dress out of the wardrobe, it looked as good as new after so many years, he asked a friend to adjust it to fit Annabelle. It did not need many adjustments. She would be proud to wear her Mother's dress for what would probably be the most important day of her life.

Chapter Five
The Wedding

The wedding day arrives at the Van Helsing household. Robert awoke early, he was excited at the prospect of marrying the most beautiful girl in the world, in his eyes.

James had stayed with them overnight in the guest bedroom. The cook started early that morning so that she could cook them all a good hearty breakfast before they go.

After breakfast; Robert, Edward, Katherine and James prepared to go to the biggest day of Robert's life. Robert was going to wear his uniform to the wedding; he looked a very handsome man in his uniform.

Meanwhile at the Calderdale household, Annabelle also awoke early, she did not sleep well thinking about her big day; she was too excited. Her Father came to her room with her dress; he held it up in front of her.

"It's beautiful!" Annabelle cried.

It was pure white with a lace trim around a low neckline, there were red silk roses stitched around the waist; stitched into the roses at the back was a long white silk train. With the dress went a white veil held on by a tiara embellished with five exquisite rubies.

Her Father sat down beside her on the bed, put his arm around her, looked at her and smiled and said "I am so happy for you my dear. I hope he will give you everything you have dreamt of and you have a long and happy life together."

"Thank you Father" she replied, with tears in her eyes.

Her Father went out of the room while she got into her dress; then she called him, he entered and stared at her so proudly.

"You're beautiful" he said, with a tear in his eye "you remind me of your Mother on our wedding day."

Time was getting on now, Robert and his Parents should be almost at the church by now.

Admiral Calderdale and Annabelle stepped outside the front door and down on the road was a coach with white ribbons all over it, Annabelle could not believe her eyes. The staff of the Calderdale household stood at the top of the steps and looked on so happy for Annabelle, for they had known her all her life.

They waved to them as they set off to the church, they had some time so the Admiral told the coachman to go the long way round to make the most of the moment. It took about thirty minutes to get to the church. Robert was already inside waiting for her to arrive, as were all their friends and relatives. The church was half full. It was a good turnout.

Then they heard the wedding march starting and knew that the beautiful bride was outside, her Father walked her slowly down the aisle, behind her were two bridesmaids, wearing pink dresses made with the finest silk. They were holding Annabelle's train up off the ground.

They reached the altar, Robert stood up and looked at Annabelle and could not believe how stunning she was and soon she was going to be his wife. The Vicar began the ceremony, they said their vows.

"We are gathered here in front of God" said the Vicar and continued "to unite these two people in holy matrimony. Do you Annabelle Calderdale take Robert Van Helsing to be your husband, to have and to hold, to love him, to cherish him till death do you part?"

"I do." Said Annabelle.

"Do you, Robert Van Helsing" the Vicar continued "take Annabelle Calderdale to be your wife, to have and to hold, to love her, to cherish her till death do you part?"

"I do." Replied Robert.

"May I have the rings?" The Vicar asked, turning to James.

James took the rings out and placed them on a pad the Vicar had held out, they were magnificent bands made from the finest welsh gold with the crests of both families etched onto each of them to signify their undying love for each other.

The Vicar held the pad in front of Robert, who picked up Annabelle's ring and proceeded to slide it onto her finger.

"Repeat after me" the Vicar said to Robert "with this ring I thee wed."

"With this ring I thee wed." Said Robert.

The Vicar then held the pad in front of Annabelle, who picked up Robert's ring and proceeded to place it onto his finger.

"Repeat after me" the Vicar reiterated "with this ring I thee wed."

"With this ring I thee wed." Said Annabelle, shaking as she was pushing the ring on Robert's finger.

"I now pronounce you Husband and Wife" the Vicar said, then continued, turning to Robert "you may kiss your Wife."

They had the most passionate kiss and the whole church erupted into cheers of joy, Annabelle had tears in her eyes again. Robert looked into them lovingly, wiping the tears away and whispering. "I love you."

After the ceremony, Robert, Annabelle and their families along with James, the best man and their friends went back to the Admiral's house where his staff had prepared a sumptuous wedding meal for them all with some wine from the cellar.

After the meal they sat down in the living room, the Admiral stood up and announced that he had a wedding present for them. He had bought them a house of their own in Southgate, North London.

They were so ecstatic, Annabelle gave her Father the biggest hug ever and they wanted to go to see it immediately, but she must get out of her wedding clothes first. They hailed a hansom cab to take them to the house. When they got there Annabelle looked at it and said "It's lovely Father, thank you." Robert also thanked him, it was more than they could ever have imagined.

"Nothing is too much for my only Daughter." Replied the Admiral.

They opened the door, which led straight into the living room with a staircase on the right, the living room led through to the dining room, which then led to the kitchen and a small garden at the back. At the top of the stairs was a landing, at the front was the master bedroom, behind that was the guest bedroom and at the rear was the bathroom with a cast iron tub on the right and a wash basin on the left wall of the room.

The house was already furnished so they decided to spend their wedding night in their new home. Annabelle and Robert went back to the Admiral's house to pick up some of Annabelle's clothes to take back to their new house.

They arrived back at the house; it was getting late now so they decided to turn in. They went upstairs to their bedroom, they started to get undressed, and Annabelle asked Robert to untie her corset at the back because she could not reach it. Robert started to untie the string on her corset, then he kissed the back of her neck and she quivered at the touch of his lips, then he turned her around and gave her the most passionate kiss on her lips, then he worked his way down, removing her corset at the same time, he kissed and caressed her breasts.

"Make love to me." Annabelle said.

Robert laid her gently on the bed then gently raised himself on top of her and they made the most exciting and passionate love yet. It seemed to last for hours, Annabelle did not want it to stop, then it came to a tremendous climax and Robert collapsed on top of Annabelle, he then rolled over and they both went to sleep in each other's arms.

Morning came and the sun was shining brightly in the sky, what a lovely day to start their married life, but this is to be short lived because Robert has to go away again very soon, the next day in fact.

They spent most of the morning in bed, making love. After lunch they went to Covent Garden market for supplies, they made the most of their time together for tomorrow Robert has to go away again.

The next morning Robert went to see the Admiral, Annabelle accompanied him, she didn't want to let go of him.

"Have you got the supplies we need, Admiral?" Robert asked.

The Admiral pointed to a large trunk in the corner of his office. "There it is" he said "you had better check it to make sure it is all there."

It was all there so he got some help to lift it down and into a coach that was going to take him to Southampton. Annabelle accompanied him to Southampton to see him off. They arrived at the Dauntless, Robert got some of his crew to take the chest on board, while he says his goodbyes to his new wife, they hugged each other, and tears came to Annabelle's eyes. "Come back safely." She said.

"Don't worry; I'll be back as soon as I can." Said Robert, then he boarded his ship.

Annabelle watched as the Dauntless set sail away from the docks, waving continuously until it disappeared into the distance, then she went to his parents house to stay for the night before going back home to their new house in London.

Annabelle entered the Van Helsing house and Katherine was sitting in the lounge, reading a book. "Come and join me." She said.

Annabelle entered the lounge and sat next to Katherine on the sofa.

Katherine saw that Annabelle was very upset so she said, trying to comfort her "don't be too sad; I am sure he will be back soon and this whole mess with the Vampires will be over."

"I know" replied Annabelle "but he is the best thing that has happened to me and I am so worried that something will happen to him."

"We think about him, also" said Katherine "but he is a big boy now and he can look after himself. I am sure that the thought of you waiting for him at home will keep him safe."

Chapter Six

The Devil's Cure

After three days at sea, the HMS. Dauntless arrived at Dr. Caruthers' island and anchored in the bay. Robert chose a crew to go with him to take the chest and the Vampire to Dr. Caruthers. They approached his house; Dr. Caruthers stepped out of the door. His eyes lit up when he caught sight of the live Vampire; he had never seen one before.

"So it is true, Vampires do exist" said Dr. Caruthers, excitedly "the blood of a Vampire would have been sufficient, but this is even better, it gives me something to experiment on."

"You will have to keep him secure" said Robert "they have extraordinary strength; if he gets loose you will be in extreme danger."

"Don't worry, I have a strong cage to keep him in" said Caruthers "and shackles that even the devil himself would not be able to escape from."

Dr. Caruthers led Robert and his men to the cage. They tethered the Vampire up in the shackles, then tossed him into the cage and locked the door to the cage.

"How long do you think you will need to develop your serum?" Asked Robert.

"I don't know" replied Caruthers "I have to carry out a lot of tests."

Robert has been instructed to stay with his crew and help Dr. Caruthers develop the cure, however long it takes.

Meanwhile late evening off the coast of Southampton, a figure appears on the horizon, its black sails fluttering in the wind. It's the Black Dahlia, stealthily nearing the sleepy port. It anchors a way out so they don't get noticed and they fly in like a swarm of bats. Once in, they spread across the town like a plague, on a feeding frenzy, but Captain Blood had his own agenda. He was in search of a particular house, the Van Helsing house. He took two of his crewmen to locate it.

After some time they found it. Captain Blood approached the house, he peered through a window, it was the living room and Edward was sitting in his chair asleep, with a book resting in his lap and a bottle of whiskey and half filled glass on a small table next to him.

Captain Blood found an open window in the study and crept in, his men followed. They crept across the hallway and up to the living room door, opened the door and crept into the living room, something startled Edward and he awoke, jumped up and turned round to see Captain Blood and two of his cronies standing there, he went for his sword which was standing in the corner, but the Vampires were too quick for him.

Captain Blood grabbed him by his arm and pulled him away from his sword, then he pulled Edward towards him. Edward reached for a cross and held it up and thrust it into Captain Blood's right cheek. Smoke emanated from it as it burnt his face and Captain Blood let out a scream and let go of Edward's arm, then Edward raced for his sword, grabbed it, pulled it out of its scabbard and spun round with it held out in front of him, but it was met by Captain Blood's sword, who knocked Edward's sword out of his hand, then Captain Blood opened his mouth revealing his fangs, pulled Edward towards him and sank his fangs deep into Edward's neck, sucking the life out of him, then Edward fell to the floor, lifeless.

Katherine was in the kitchen, she heard a noise in the living room so she went to investigate and she saw Edward lying there with Captain Blood and his men standing over him.

She screamed. "What have you done?"

"Grab her!" Captain Blood ordered. "We'll take her with us."

Captain Blood's henchmen grabbed hold of her, but she wasn't going quietly, she was kicking and screaming, then they disappeared into the night. They got back to their ship, and then faded away into the distance, leaving bodies strewn around the streets of Southampton in their wake.

Back on Caruthers' island, Dr. Caruthers shouted "I think I have found it!"

Robert and James ran into the room "does it work?" Asked Robert.

"I don't know yet" replied Caruthers "I will have to test it on our Vampire."

He filled a syringe with the formula and they went to the cage they were holding the Vampire. He told some of the natives to hold the Vampire down, then plunged the syringe into his arm and emptied it. They waited a while for it to work, then all of a sudden the Vampire started convulsing, so everyone exited the cage for their own safety, because they did not understand what was happening. The Vampire fell to the ground, doubled up and shaking like he was having a fit. This lasted for fifteen minutes, and then he was still.

"Is he dead?" Asked James.

"I don't know" replied Caruthers "he doesn't look too well."

Robert volunteered to go into the cage to find out. He opened the door, stepped in, knelt down and put his hand around the Vampire's wrist. "He has a pulse." Robert said, turning to Caruthers and James.

Just then the Vampire reeled back in shock. "What's happening?" He said. "Where am I?" He turned to Robert and said. "Who are you?"

"Do you remember anything?" Said Robert. "What's your name, where do you come from, anything that has happened to you up to now."

"I don't remember anything" said the Vampire "the last thing I remember was on my ship and then we were being attacked by Pirates. After that, there is nothing until now."

Robert asked him to open his mouth, which he did and there was no sign of any fangs. Robert turned to Dr. Caruthers and said "I think you have done it, I think he is human again."

The Vampire looked at Robert as if he was mad and said. "What do you mean human. Again?"

"You were a Vampire" Robert said "but we have cured you."

"A Vampire?" He said. "Are you insane? I didn't think there were any such things."

"You must come with us." Said Robert.

Robert told Dr. Caruthers to pack all the serum he has made, they will take it with them, then they carried it to the Dauntless and set sail for home.

Three days later, they were approaching Southampton harbour, their happiness was to be short lived, for when they docked they saw there was something wrong. Robert and James went ashore and saw numerous wooden boxes lining the street.

He stopped a passing lady and said. "What is happening here? What are all these boxes?"

"Have you not heard?" She said. "Where have you been. We were attacked by Vampires, they killed hundreds of people. It was like hell and damnation. These are coffins."

The lids to the coffins were not nailed down, so Robert opened everyone of them in turn to see if there was anyone he knew, which there wasn't, then he stood there for a second and then a thought sprang to his mind. Are his parents alright? He turned to James and said. "We must get to my parents' house."

They set off to Robert's parents' house, they reached the front door, it was ajar. There is something not right here. Robert cautiously pushed it open and stepped inside. He called out and was met with silence, James went to look upstairs and Robert walked towards the living room. The door was open so he went in he spotted a pair of legs from behind the chair. He ran round the chair and saw his Father lying there as white as a sheet, he was dead. Robert fell to his knees by the side of his Father, sobbing; he lifted his Father's lifeless body and cradled it in his arms.

James walked in and saw Robert there with his Father. "I am so sorry." He said.

"Did you find my Mother?" Asked Robert.

"No" replied James "she is nowhere in the house, perhaps they have taken her."

Robert stood up and turned towards the door. James saw the anger in his eyes, it could only be bad. He knew Robert was going to go after Captain Blood and in that mood he will endanger the whole crew, so James stood in his way.

"You can't go after him in this frame of mind." Said James.

"Get out of my way!" Shouted Robert, holding aloft his sword "or I will run you through."

"No" said James "you don't know what you are doing. I am telling you as your First Mate and your friend; in this frame of mind you will get us all killed, including your Mother. If they have her, she will be the first one they will kill. Go home to your wife for a couple of days until you calm down, then we will go and get your Mother back and make Captain Blood pay."

"Very well" said Robert, calming down "you're right, we must have a plan. You are a good friend, James."

Robert made a pyre out in the back garden, with the help of James and then he and James carried Edward's body out, put it on the pyre and set alight to it. They stood there and said a prayer while the body was being cremated.

It was getting late so Robert and James stayed there for the night.

Robert did not sleep at all well again. It seems that his Father was right about his family being cursed and now he has to try to break the curse by defeating Captain Blood.

The next morning Robert and James took a coach to London. Robert got out at his home, where Annabelle was waiting for him and James carried on to see Admiral Calderdale to update him.

Robert stepped in the door, Annabelle ran up to him, swung her arms around him and kissed him, then she noticed there was something wrong.

"What's wrong?" She said.

"It's my Father." Said Robert.

"What's wrong with him?" Enquired Annabelle.

"He is dead" said Robert "Southampton was attacked by Vampires when we were away. They killed my Father, and my Mother is missing. We think they have her."

"Oh, I am so sorry" said Annabelle "what are you going to do?"

"I am going to get her back and make Captain Blood and all his Vampires pay for what they have done."

"Be careful" said Annabelle "I have some news to tell you, but I don't know if this is the right time."

"Is it good news or bad?" Asked Robert.

"Good." Said Annabelle.

"Then tell me it now" said Robert "it might cheer me up a bit."

"I am with child." Said Annabelle, excitedly.

"What do you mean?" Asked Robert, as if he didn't know.

"I am expecting a baby." Said Annabelle.

Robert sat down, a bit shocked, and then a smile came to his face. "That's excellent." He said. He stood up and gave Annabelle the biggest hug and kissed her on her lips, they just stood in that position for about ten minutes.

Later on, James came to their house; he was staying there for the night. They had a sumptuous dinner that Annabelle had cooked for them, then after dinner they retired to the living room for an aperitif. Robert told James the news about the baby; James was almost as delighted as Robert. "Congratulations" he said "you deserve some good luck for a change."

"I would like to make a toast to both of you." Said James.

"Thank you" said Robert "we would like you to be the Godfather."

James was over the moon "I would be honoured." He said.

"Good, then let us drink a toast to that." Said Robert. At this rate they will be drunk before the night is out.

The next morning arrived, the sun was beating down. After breakfast, Robert and James went to see the Admiral.

"Has Annabelle told you the news?" Robert asked Admiral Calderdale.

"Yes. Congratulations" replied the Admiral "does this mean I am going to be a Grandfather."

"Yes, I am afraid so, but there is also some bad news" said Robert, his face turning serious "my Father has been killed, probably by Captain Blood's own hand, and my Mother is missing. I think he has her."

"Yes I know. James informed me yesterday. I am sorry to hear that" said Admiral Calderdale "do you want to take some time off to mourn?"

"No" said Robert "I want to find them and get my Mother back, hopefully alive."

"I think if he was going to kill her, he would have done it straight away." Said the Admiral.

James piped up. "You're right, maybe he needs her for something."

"Maybe he wants her to get to me" said Robert "I won't disappoint him. As soon as we have stocked up with our supplies we will set sail."

Robert and James left the Admiralty and went back to Robert's house, he wanted to spend a bit of time with Annabelle before going to sea because he knew it was going to be a long and dangerous mission and he did not know when he will return, if at all. He just hopes to return before the birth of his child.

The sun rose on a glorious morning, Robert and James had a hearty breakfast before setting off on their perilous journey. They said their goodbyes to a tearful Annabelle.

"Come back safely" she said, hopefully "both of you."

Chapter Seven
The Final Battle

Robert and James climbed into a coach that was waiting outside for them and set off to Southampton to join their ship. Once aboard the Dauntless, they made sure they had everything they need before they set sail. They want to leave nothing to chance.

"Anchors aweigh!" Ordered Captain Robert Van Helsing. "Full sail ahead."

"Have we any news as to their whereabouts?" Robert asked James Turner.

"They were last seen south of the Caribbean" replied James, then pointed to a spot on the map "there are a group of islands in the South Atlantic, perhaps they will be anchored there."

Captain Morgan was looking over their shoulders and piped up "I know these islands, I have been there. There is treasure buried on one of them, but I don't know which one. There is no map."

"How do you know this?" Asked Robert.

"Because we followed it there. It is the treasure of the Conquistadors." Replied Captain Morgan.

"I have heard of that" said James "there is more treasure than you can imagine, so they say."

"They are right" replied Captain Morgan and with a look of lust in his eyes added "I have seen it. I have touched it. It is real."

"Come down below and tell me the story." Said Robert, leading Captain Morgan down to his cabin.

Once in the Captain's quarters, Robert walked to his drinks cabinet, opened the doors and removed from it a bottle of rum and two glasses. He placed the glasses on his table and proceeded to fill them with the rum, then picked them up and handed one to Captain Morgan.

"So, how do you know so much about this treasure?" Asked Robert, inquisitively.

"We found it" explained Captain Morgan "we had a map of the treasure and we followed the map to a place called the Devil's Triangle, where all manner of evil resides. A lot of ships and their crews have perished there. We were being pursued by the Navy, a man by the name of Captain George Meriwether, and by another Pirate, Captain Blackbeard. We found the treasure, but then we were surprised by Captain Meriwether and his men. They got away with the treasure and we tracked them to these islands where they must have buried it, because it wasn't on their ship."

"What happened to Captain Meriwether?" Asked Robert.

"He is dead" replied Captain Morgan "I killed him because he killed my Captain in cold blood. We searched his ship inside and out, but never found the treasure."

"That's an interesting story" said Robert, looking fascinated "maybe when we have killed all of the Vampires and made the world safe, we can search for the treasure."

Robert and William Morgan finished their drinks and then went back on deck.

The morning of the sixth day came. The lookout in the crows nest cried "Land ahoy!"

Robert lifted his spyglass up to his eye and looked through it. "It looks like we have found the islands, but there is no sign of the Black Dahlia." Said Robert.

"Maybe it is at one of the other islands." Replied Captain Morgan.

"We will circle around them. Look out for any hidden coves" ordered Robert "we don't want to be surprised."

There were four small islands in the group. They neared them slowly on half sail and when they got as close as they could without grounding, they turned to starboard to go around the first island. Everyone's eyes were peeled in case of a possible ambush. They saw a hidden bay and decided to enter it, they dropped anchor in the bay, there were mountains all around them and Robert decided to take a party ashore and try to get to the top of the mountains where they can get a better view of the whole area, Captain Morgan volunteered to go with them, he didn't want to miss out if they stumbled on the treasure.

They rowed their boat ashore and pulled it up onto the beach. They noticed footsteps in the sand, so they followed them into a valley between the mountains. As they came to the end of the valley, there was a dense forest. They made their way slowly through the thicket, until they came to the end of the forest, where they saw a village of mud huts. Robert took out his spyglass and looked through it; he saw that there was no movement at all in the village, so he decided to investigate.

He took Captain Morgan and three other men with him and crept down to the village and still they saw no movement.

"It looks like there is nobody here." Said Captain Morgan.

"Perhaps not" replied Robert "but we must make sure."

Robert walked up to the first hut and put his head through the doorway and then pulled it out again, looking like he was in shock, his eyes staring into space.

"What's wrong?" Asked Captain Morgan. "You don't look too well."

"Look in there." Said Robert, pointing to the doorway.

Captain Morgan peered through the door and saw what seemed to be a whole family of natives scattered around the hut, dead.

"Shiver me timbers!" Exclaimed Captain Morgan, as he entered the hut. "It looks like they are all dead." He knelt down to one of the bodies and tilted the head to one side. "Look at these marks on the neck" he said "it looks like our Vampires were here."

They then walked around the whole village, entering evey hut in turn and were encountered by the same situation. A whole village slaughtered by the Vampires. Robert beckoned the rest of his men that were waiting at the edge of the forest into the village

"We have to find a way to the top of the mountain" said Robert "we have to find these animals, but first we have to burn the corpses in case they turn, otherwise we will have more trouble than we can handle."

They made sure there was nobody left alive, then set alight to each hut in turn. When the village was well alight, they departed to look for a way up the mountain.

Ahead of them was what looked to be a pathway winding up the mountain, so they proceeded to ascend. It was a long haul, but they eventually reached the summit, from where they could see for miles around the islands. If the Vampires were anywhere in the area, they will see them.

Robert took out his spyglass and put it up to his eye. He looked to the north, he looked to the east, then the south and finally the west, then something caught his eye and he looked back to the south.

"There is someone down there on the south island." Said Robert.

"Can I have a look?" Captain Morgan asked, taking the spyglass. "That looks like them, but where is their ship?"

"They must have it hidden in some secluded bay" replied Robert "we must get back to our ship and go after them, but remember they have probably got my Mother on board, so we have to proceed with caution."

They descended back down the mountain and through the forest the way they came, on to the beach and into their boats and back to their ship.

James Turner was standing on the poop deck. "Did you find anything?" He asked.

"We know where they are" Robert replied "they are on the south island."

They made their way slowly around the island towards the south island, trying to keep out of sight. Robert kept his spyglass fixed to his eye to see if he can spot the Black Dahlia.

"There is a bay ahead" said Robert "I can see a mast above the rocks; turn to port so I can get a better sight of it."

They moved to a better position. "That's it!" Cried Robert. "I can see the black sails and it looks like most of the crew are ashore."

They saw their chance to rescue Katherine, Robert's Mother. They anchored out of sight and lowered two boats into the water, and then Robert and some of his most hardened men, including James Turner and Captain Morgan and his men scaled down into the boats and rowed stealthily towards the Black Dahlia.

Upon reaching the Dahlia, Captain Morgan rowed to the other side of the ship, then they launched grappling hooks up the sides and scaled up to the deck, keeping their heads down. Robert drew his sword and ordered his men to do the same, then looked around on the deck. There were six Vampires visible, he signalled to Morgan to take the three on their side.

When the Vampires were close enough, Robert and his men leapt onto the deck and, likewise, Captain Morgan and his men. As Robert landed on the deck, the Vampire nearest to him turned around looking Robert straight in the face and Robert lifted his sword, swung it at head height and took the Vampire's head clean off, then the Vampire turned to dust, the rest of the men did the same with little resistance.

"Check the deck" ordered Robert "ensure there are no more Vampires on deck."

After clearing the deck, Robert looked at his men and pointed to two of them. "You and you" he ordered "stay here on lookout and let us know if any Vampires leave the island, we will go down below to look for my Mother."

They descended down the steps towards the cabins, looking around so that there are no surprises. Ahead of them was the door to the Captain's quarters. Robert walked up to the door, opened it and walked into the room, followed by the rest of the men. Robert looked to his left and there, sitting on a bench seat, was Katherine, with her back towards them.

"Mother!" Shouted Robert.

Katherine turned round and replied "Hello Robert."

Then she rose to her feet and they held their arms open and went into each other's arms and hugged, tightly.

As they were in the embrace, Katherine was facing Captain Morgan and she opened her mouth.

"Captain!" Said Morgan. "I think you had better part, there is something wrong."

Robert let go of Katherine and she did likewise, he looked back at Captain Morgan. "What do mean?" He said.

"Look around." Said Morgan.

Robert turned round towards Katherine and reeled back, she has fangs. Captain Blood has turned her into a Vampire.

"No!" Screamed Robert, reeling back. "Not you too."

Just then, there was a scream outside the cabin. Robert and Morgan looked round and one of the men they left on guard staggered in with a sword right through his stomach, who then fell to the floor. Behind him was Captain Blood and his Vampires bearing muskets, they had been hiding at the other end of the ship. It seems that they were expecting them.

"Hello Robert" said Captain Blood "I told you we will meet again."

"How do you know my name?" Asked Robert.

"I should know the name of my Nephew." Replied Captain Blood.

"What do you mean Nephew?" Said Robert, surprised.

Captain Blood turned to Katherine. "You haven't told him that I am your Brother." He said.

"No" said Katherine "I wanted to protect him."

"So, Robert" said Captain Blood "now you know your Mother is a Vampire, why don't you join us?"

"Never!" Demanded Robert.

"Think about it, Robert" said Katherine "he could make you immortal."

Katherine held out her arms to take Robert in an embrace, she wrapped her arms around him and opened her mouth to reveal her fangs.

Robert reached down to his waist, pulled a syringe out that he had tucked away in his belt and embedded it into his Mother's neck, then emptied it. She let out a sharp yelp, then collapsed on the floor and started writhing around in agony, then laid still.

"What have you done to her?" Said Captain Blood. "Have you killed her?"

"No" replied Robert "I have just undone what you did; I have turned her back into a mortal."

"I don't believe you" said Captain Blood "it cannot be done."

Robert knelt down by Katherine's side and felt her neck for a pulse, and then her eyes opened slowly.

"What happened?" Said Katherine, looking up at Robert. "Where am I?"

Robert pulled Katherine's head up and cradled it in his arms. "Welcome back, Mother." He said, emotionally.

"Robert?" Katherine seemed surprised to see him. "I thought you were at sea."

"We are at sea" replied Robert "do you not remember anything?"

"The last thing I remember is sitting at home with Edward" said Katherine "where is he?"

"I am sorry mother, but he is dead" said Robert, hesitantly "he was killed by Vampires."

"Oh no" cried Katherine, sobbing and then she looked up at Captain Blood, still confused and said "Henry, what are you doing here? I thought you were dead."

"He is" said Robert "he is a Vampire; he is the thing that killed Father."

"No!" Said Katherine. "Henry wouldn't do that."

"He is not your Brother anymore, Mother" said Robert "he is a Vampire."

"Is this true?" Katherine asked, looking at Captain Blood.

Captain Blood did not answer that question, but looked at his men and ordered "Take them away, all of them. Lock them in the hold; we will deal with them later."

Captain Blood's men tossed them in the hold and locked the heavy oak door behind them.

"I still can't believe my Brother would do this to us" said Katherine "what are they going to do to us?"

"They are keeping us for dinner." Said Captain Morgan, attempting to raise the mood.

"Mind what you say" said Robert "my Mother has gone through enough. We have to find a way out of this."

Robert tried the door, but to no avail. It was a heavy duty door, and then Captain Morgan tried with his brute strength, still to no avail. They were walking up and down trying to think how to get out before the Vampires come back; then Katherine walked up to the door and gave a tug on the handle and the door came off its hinges in her hand. The men stared at her in amazement.

"How did you do that?" Said Captain Morgan.

"I don't know" replied Katherine "I just pulled it and it came off."

"I think I know what's happened" said James, looking at Robert "when you injected her with the serum, you made her mortal again, but she must have kept her Vampire strength."

"We can work this out later" said Captain Morgan "right now we have to get out of here before we end up as the Vampires' main course."

Robert poked his head out of the doorway and looked left then right. "There are no guards" he said "they must have thought we would not be able to open the door."

"How are we going to fight the Vampires without weapons?" Asked James.

"We are not" replied Robert "we will get back to our ship and re-arm, then come back and destroy them."

"How will we get past the Vampires on deck?" Asked James.

"We will find a way" replied Robert "we will deal with one problem at a time."

They found some rope in the hold; they could use it to scale down the ship. Robert led the way, he crept towards the Captain's quarters, put his ear to the door. He could hear nothing, so he pushed the door open slightly to look inside. The room was empty, so they entered it. Robert went to the windows and looked out.

"Our boats are still tied to the ship." He said, and then tied one end of the rope to a sturdy beam. "We will climb down the rope, into the water and swim to the boats. Captain Morgan will go first, then my Mother and then the rest of us. I will go last and make sure nobody come in." He ordered.

They descended down the rope, one by one, into the water and swam quietly to the boats, then climbed in, untied them and started rowing away from the Black Dahlia.

"Captain!" Shouted a lookout on the Dahlia, pointing over the side of the ship. "The prisoners have escaped."

"Man the starboard guns." Captain Blood ordered.

They had sixteen guns on each side of the ship and they fired all of the starboard guns in sequence at the boats, narrowly missing them, but throwing waves over them and rocking the boats from left to right, almost capsizing them.

Robert and his men reached the Dauntless in one piece, then climbed up the ropes and boarded her. They were greeted by the rest of the crew.

"Man the guns" ordered Robert "get ready to fire on my word."

The Dauntless turned and pointed towards the Black Dahlia, then headed straight for it. When they got within range, the Dahlia fired its guns which landed in the water either side of the Dauntless, sending water fifty feet high, washing over the deck of the Dauntless, putting some of the crew off their feet.

As the Dauntless neared the Dahlia, Robert gave the order to turn hard to port so that they were broadside of the Dahlia, and then gave the order to fire.

All the guns blasted and they went straight through the ghost ship with no effect, then Robert thought it a pointless exercise, so he decided that they were going to board the Dahlia. They headed straight for the Dahlia and when they got as close as possible, they veered hard to port so that they hit the Dahlia, broadside, then almost the whole crew of the Dauntless swung over to the Black Dahlia on ropes, leaving only a skeleton crew aboard the Dauntless.

"Fight like you've never fought before" ordered Robert "leave nothing alive, but for Captain Blood. He is mine."

As they went over to the Dahlia, a handful of the Dahlia's crew swung over to the Dauntless to recapture Katherine, but they did not reckon on the strength she acquired when Captain Blood turned her into a Vampire.

The crew on the Dauntless were holding the Vampires off. They now know how to kill them. Three of the Vampires proceeded down below to search for Katherine, who was sitting in one of the cabins, unaware that she was being sought by the Vampires.

They slowly and cautiously opened one door at a time, until they came to the Captain's quarters. The leading Vampire pushed the door and was met by the end of a sword with a shining silver blade thrust straight through his heart and Katherine at the other end of it.

The Vampire disintegrated into a pile of ash on the floor. The next Vampire leapt forward to grab Katherine, but she was too quick for him and grasped him arm, swung him around, let go and he flew through the window and into the sea below.

The final Vampire stood forward and all of a sudden just disintegrated and standing behind was one of Robert's men with his sword held aloft.

"Thank you." Said Katherine, exhausted.

"It's my pleasure Mrs. Van Helsing" he replied "it is my job."

It was a hard fought battle back on the Dahlia, there were muskets blasting, swords clattering and everyone was watching each other's backs. Nobody had a clue what had just occurred aboard the Dauntless.

Robert saw James with his back to the wall and three Vampires confronting him, so he Took hold of a rope and swung across with his sword held aloft and swooped down onto them and with one action of his sword, he took off the heads of two of them and they turned to ash, then James picked up his sword while the other one was looking away and pierced him straight through the heart and he too turned to ash at James's feet, then they carried on fighting to rid the ship of the Vampires.

After a long and bloody battle, all the Vampires on the deck were turned to ash, but in all the confusion, Robert had forgotten about Captain Blood.

"Has anyone seen Captain Blood?" Asked Robert.

Everyone answered at the same time. "No, Captain!"

Robert ordered his men to search the ship from top to bottom until they find him. He must not get away. They stayed in groups of four or five. Robert led one group, Captain Morgan another and James Turner another.

"If anyone finds him, let me know" said Robert "he's mine."

They searched high and low for him, but with no success, then James heard a sound coming from the galley. He told one of his men to go and get Robert, whilst they waited outside the door to the galley.

Robert arrived. "Have you found him?" He asked.

"I might have" replied James "I heard a noise in the hold."

Robert pushed the door open slowly, held his sword up in front of him, then put his head through the doorway, and then stepped into the galley, cautiously, followed by his men. They carefully searched the galley, moving items in case Captain Blood was hiding behind them. There was no sign of him. Then all of a sudden, something dropped down from above. It was Captain Blood; he was hiding in the rafters. He got hold of one of the men and put his sword straight through him, then another.

"Everyone stand down!" Ordered Robert. "I will deal with this one."

Robert approached Captain Blood with his sword aloft, they crossed sword, and then the swordfight began. They went on for ten minutes with neither of them gaining the advantage.

"You fight well" Captain Blood said to Robert "but do you fight well enough to defeat me?"

"We shall see." Replied Robert, then Robert swung his sword across Captain Blood's chest and put a gash in it, but then it just seemed to heal itself, almost immediately.

"You're Father taught you well." Said Captain Blood.

"My Father didn't teach me" replied Robert "the Navy taught me."

They carried on fighting for another fifteen minutes, then Robert took the initiative and knocked Captain Blood's sword from his hands, then pinned him up against the wall with his sword pointed at Captain Blood's heart.

"Can you do it?" Said Captain Blood. "Can you slay your own Uncle?"

"You are not my Uncle" replied Robert "my Uncle is dead. You are just evil inside my Uncle's body and I owe you for what you did to my Father."

Captain Blood smiled at Robert, then Robert pushed his sword harder and harder, and then ran it through Captain

Blood's heart as hard as he could and Captain Blood's face turned from a smile to intense agony and he seemed to be ageing ten years every second, then he turned to ash.

Robert stood back and just stared at the space that Captain Blood previously occupied. James Turner walked up behind Robert and placed his hand on his shoulder, but he still stood there, staring.

"He wasn't your Uncle anymore." Said James, consoling him.

"It's done" said Robert "it's all over."

Just then, a fire suddenly appeared from nowhere, then another and another.

"We have to get out of here" said Robert "the ship is dying."

They scrambled out of the hold and up to the deck. By this time, there were fires all over the ship. They all grabbed a rope and swung back over to the Dauntless, then turned around to watch as the Black Dahlia burnt. It was now an inferno, flames were rising high into the sky, then the bow dipped under the water and the rest of the ship followed until the ship was gone, into the deep.

Katherine ran up to the deck, bustled her way through the men until she reached Robert, held out her arms and wrapped them around Robert.

"Don't squeeze so hard, Mother" said Robert "remember you still have the strength of a Vampire."

"I am so glad that you are safe" she said "where is the Black Dahlia?"

"It's gone." Replied Robert.

"What about Henry?" Said Katherine.

"He is dead" Robert replied "I killed him. He wasn't your Brother anymore, he was a Vampire that killed him and took his body and he killed my Father."

"Are we going after the treasure now that the world is safe?" Said Captain Morgan.

"I will have to think about it" replied Robert "it has been a long day. We will drop anchor here for the night and I will decide in the morning. Tomorrow is a new day."

Robert took his Mother down below to the Captain's quarters, where he saw ash all over the floor.

"What is this?" He asked Katherine.

Katherine replied. "Some Vampires came aboard and tried to take me, but we killed them. One of your men saved my life."

"I will have to give him my gratitude" Said Robert "now we must rest. After we have found this treasure, we will go home happy with the knowledge that the world is now a safer place, although we have made a lot of sacrifices. We owe a lot to the men that have perished at the hands of these evil creatures."

Morning arrived; the sun was high in the sky. It would be a nice day for treasure hunting. Robert went up on deck; Captain Morgan was standing at the bow looking out to sea, so Robert went to join him.

"Which island do you think the treasure is on?" Asked Robert.

"When we found Captain Meriwether, they were anchored off the west island." Replied Captain Morgan.

"Good, then we will start there" said Robert "but if we don't find it before the day is out, then we will go home without it."

They anchored the Dauntless off the north coast of the west island and lowered two boats into the water, then climbed down into them and rowed ashore. They pulled the boats up onto the sand and split into three groups; it would be quicker. Robert led one group, James another and

Captain Morgan the other. Robert led his group southwards; James went eastwards and Morgan westwards.

Before they set off, Robert ordered "If anyone should find something, they are to fire a shot and we will meet back here."

Robert and his group had to negotiate a dense forest. They found a path which looked like it had been flattened, either by Captain Meriwether or natives, hopefully Meriwether. They made their way through the forest until they reached the end, where there was a vast plain, beyond which was a mountain range.

Meanwhile, James and his men were making their way around the coast until they could not go any further. They reached an inlet and on the other side of the inlet was what looked like a cave which could only be reached by boat.

"That looks like a likely place to hide treasure" James said to his men "we must signal to the others."

He drew his musket and fired in the air to let the other groups know, and then they made their way back to the boats.

They all met back at the boats.

"What have you found?" Robert asked James.

"There is a cave at the other side of that bay" James replied, pointing to the inlet in the distance "maybe the treasure is in there."

"Man the boats" ordered Robert "we will see if the treasure is in there. We have nothing to lose."

They climbed into their boats and rowed around the island to the inlet and across to the cave. As they proceeded deeper into the cave, the passage seemed to be getting narrower and it was getting so dark that they could hardly see so they lit up some torches. The cave seemed endless, until they saw a glimmering light ahead of them and the passage seemed to open up again.

As they got closer, they saw that it was not a light, but a reflection from their torches, for in front of them was a mound of treasure on a sandbank; the like of which they had never seen before, except, of course, Captain Morgan and what's left of his men, for they were the ones that found it, then ultimately lost it.

The men could not believe what they were seeing, they ran up to it, picked some of it up and ran it through their fingers, over their heads as if they were showering in it, they were like men possessed.

"That's enough playing around" ordered Robert, not at all perturbed by the sight he was witnessing "we must get this back to the ship so we can go home."

They gathered all of the treasure, not dropping even one piece of it and piled it up in the boats, but there was so much that they needed more than one trip, which took a lot of time.

Once all the treasure was aboard, they locked it in the hold and Robert gave the order to weigh anchor and set sail, they are going home. It was going to be a long journey. Robert can't wait to see his beloved Annabelle.

The second day of their voyage home, Robert was standing at the bow of the ship, looking out to sea and Captain Morgan joined him.

"Now that it is all over, what is going to happen to me?" Captain Morgan asked.

"I don't know, but I will speak up for you" replied Robert "you have been invaluable to me. If you tell them your whole story of how you became a Pirate, they may take that into account and look on it sympathetically. I met the Judges at my Father-in-law's New Year party and they seem to be good people. I am sure that you will receive a fair hearing."

"What about the treasure?" Asked Captain Morgan.

"I will have to let the Admiral know about it, but your main concern should be what is going to happen to yourself." Said Robert.

"It seems such a waste." Said Captain Morgan.

"I can't risk hiding it from the authorities" said Robert "I have a lovely wife and a child on the way."

Eight days later, they reached the docks at Southampton. As they embarked, each man kissed the ground, thankful that they have arrived home safely and spared a thought for those that didn't.

Robert ordered James to stay and guard the treasure while he took Captain Morgan and his men to see the Admiral in London. Upon reaching the Admiralty, they went to see Admiral Calderdale.

"Welcome Robert" said the Admiral "how did it go, did you find Captain Blood?"

"It is all over" replied Robert "they are all dead and my Mother is safe."

"Well done" said the Admiral "what about Captain Morgan?"

"He is outside in your reception with his men." Replied Robert.

"They will have to go back to prison" said the Admiral "at least until their hearing."

"I would like to speak on their behalf" said Robert "they have been invaluable to me in my struggle against evil and I would like to have them in my crew."

"Do you think that is wise?" Asked the Admiral.

"I trust him with my life" replied Robert "indeed, he saved my life on numerous occasions."

"I don't know if I can do it" said the Admiral "but I will put it to the council. Come and see me tomorrow, now you must go and be with your wife, she will be pleased to see you. We will keep Captain Morgan here until then."

"There is another thing" said Robert "we recovered some treasure while we were there."

"What treasure?" Asked the Admiral.

"It is the treasure of the conquistadors." Replied Robert.

"I have heard of that treasure" said the Admiral "it was lost a hundred years ago. As far as I know it belongs to nobody now, but I will check on it and let you know."

Robert left the Admiralty and went home to Annabelle. He opened the door and was met by his wife who ran to him with her arms outstretched, wrapped them around him and squeezed him tight. She was so happy to see him safe and well.

"Be careful!" Said Robert, looking worried "you shouldn't be rushing around in your condition." He looked at her and said. "You're looking big now."

"Yes" she said "I am expecting to have it within the next two weeks."

The next day, Robert went to see Admiral Calderdale to get the answers to his questions.

"I have asked the council about Captain Morgan" said the Admiral "they can't let him go, but they can have a hearing where you can speak on his behalf. Maybe it will get him a reprieve; it will take place next Thursday, at noon."

"That seems fair to me" said Robert "what about the treasure?"

"I have checked up on that and I was right" replied the Admiral "it belongs to whoever finds it, which, it seems, is you and your crew. It seems that you are rich men."

"That is very good news" said Robert "the men will be pleased. I think they have earned it."

Robert left the Admiralty and went home to his wife. He told her all about his exploits, also about the treasure and the fact that he has to go to the hearing for Captain Morgan.

"Are we rich?" Asked Annabelle, excitedly.

"We will not have to worry about money again." Robert replied.

Annabelle looked down at her large stomach and said "did you hear that, son?"

"How do you know it is going to be a boy?" Robert asked.

Annabelle replied "I don't. I just hope it is, for you."

"I don't mind if it is a boy or a girl" Robert replied "as long as it is healthy."

They went to the lounge to relax. The midwife was there and she made a pot of tea, brought it in and placed it on the table. "This will do you good." She said.

The day of the hearing arrives. Robert goes to the Admiralty, where the hearing is to take place. He entered the courtroom and sat down in the witnesses area. A few minutes later, three men walked in and sat down behind the bench, they were the panel of Judges that would decide Captain Morgan's fate along with his men.

"Bring in the prisoners!" The usher cried.

Captain Morgan and his men were then led into the dock, where they stood while the court clerk read out their names and they all answered to them, then they were instructed to sit down.

The lead Judge spoke up "Captain William Morgan and his crew were found guilty of piracy on the high seas and sentenced to hang by the gallows, but it was requested by a Captain Robert Van Helsing that they join him in his quest and destruction of creatures called Vampires, which they did to great effect. We have heard about their conduct in this matter and decided to grant them this hearing to decide their fate. Who will speak on the prisoners' behalf?"

Robert arose from the witnesses bench and said "I will."

"Very well." Said the lead Judge, and then began. "The prisoners stood accused of piracy on the high seas and indeed were found guilty and sentenced to hang, but they were saved from the gallows because Captain Robert Van Helsing needed them for a mission of vital importance to the world. For this they were spared the gallows, but they still have to pay for their crimes against humanity. As we gather, Captain Van Helsing wishes to speak on their behalf to quash their sentences. Let the case begin."

The usher called out "I call Captain Robert Van Helsing to the stand."

Robert took the stand and started his speech. "When I asked Admiral Calderdale for permission to take Captain Morgan and his men, I did not think they would come back alive and I thought it would be no loss, but getting to know him, I think he is a changed man. He was invaluable to us in the struggle against the Vampires. In fact, I don't think we could have completed our mission without him. He saved my life on numerous occasions and I have never seen anyone fight with such passion for his comrades. They will be a big asset in our fight against the French. I would like to beg the panel to give Captain Morgan and his crew another chance and release them into my custody. I will be totally responsible for them. If they cross me, I will personally hunt them down to the ends of the earth. There is also something I think you should hear from Captain Morgan about how he became a Pirate. It is an unfortunate story. That is all your Honour."

"Very well" said the lead Judge, then added "you may stand down. Call Captain Morgan to the stand."

Captain Morgan walked up and stood in the dock to tell his story. He left nothing out, how his Father abused both him and his Mother for all those years and that he killed his Father in a fit of temper because his Father killed his Mother without even a hint of remorse.

There were whispers going around the gallery of the courtroom. Some of the women were in tears at what they were hearing and the men were looking saddened at his heart rendering story. They could certainly sympathise with it, maybe the Judges will.

The three Judges whispered among themselves for a moment, then the lead Judge said. "That was a good speech in defense of the prisoners and a sad tale of woe from Captain Morgan, but we cannot decide at this moment in time. You may stand down. This court will adjourn until two o'clock. Take the prisoners back to the cells until then."

The courtroom emptied and Robert sat on a bench outside. Admiral Calderdale walked up and sat next to him. "That was a good speech, Robert." He said.

"I meant every word it." Replied Robert.

"I think you may have made a good case for them and with a little bit of luck, who knows." Said the Admiral.

Two o'clock came and the courtroom filled again. Every one stood up when the Judges entered the room. "All be seated." Ordered the usher.

The lead Judge stood up and said. "Captain Van Helsing is a distinguished figure in our Royal Navy and he has had high praise from Admiral Calderdale."

After deliberating and taking into account everything that has been said in this courtroom, we have decided to give Captain Morgan and his crew a conditional pardon on condition that they will be in the custody of Captain Van Helsing, but if they dishonour their pardon, Captain Van Helsing will be liable and charged with bringing them to justice by any means possible. The prisoners are free to go. Court closed."

There were shouts of joy from the dock and a smile on Robert's face. Captain Morgan went to Robert and shook his hand. "Thank you Captain" he said "I owe you my life."

"You deserve another chance. Just do not disappoint me." Robert replied.

The next day, Robert had to get back to the Dauntless. He took Captain Morgan and company with him and the rest of the crew were happy to see them, then he told them that the treasure is all theirs and they were overjoyed. They shared it out equally among them, even with Captain Morgan and his men, because they earned it no matter what they did in the past. Robert found a magnificent Ruby and Diamond brooch and picked it up. "Annabelle will love this." He said to himself.

The next minute, a man rushed in and looked around the room. "Captain Van Helsing?" He enquired.

"That's me." Replied Robert.

"You are needed in London" the man said "it's your wife, you must come quickly. I have horses waiting outside."

Robert went with the man; they sped to London on the horses as fast as their legs could carry them. They arrived at Robert's house, opened the door and were met by Admiral Calderdale.

"Annabelle has gone into labour." He said.

"Is everything alright?" Asked Robert, looking worried.

"Yes, the midwife is with her now in the bedchamber" said the Admiral "Annabelle has been asking for you."

Robert rushed upstairs to the bedroom and entered. The midwife was there just about to deliver the baby. Robert went to Annabelle and held her hand. She looked at Robert and a smile came to her face, then she squeezed his hand so tight that it stopped the circulation.

"Push!" Shouted the midwife.

Annabelle let out a scream as she tried to push the baby out.

"Push again!" The midwife repeated.

Annabelle let out another scream as she pushed even harder; then the midwife saw a head protruding and helped ease the baby out as Annabelle continued pushing for glory, then out it came and let out a cry.

"It' a boy!" Said the midwife. "Congratulations."

"I am still in pain!" Cried Annabelle.

The midwife laid the baby boy on a blanket and went back to have a look and she saw another head protruding out. "You have another one." She said, in amazement, so she gently got hold of it and told Annabelle to start pushing again. Annabelle continued pushing and screaming until it came out. Robert had to leave the room whilst this was going on before he went deaf for they were ear piercing screams.

"This one is a girl" she said "I had better make sure there are no others. No that's all there is."

The midwife then called Robert back to Annabelle's side.

"You have twins" Said the midwife "one boy and one girl. I have never experienced this before. It is amazing."

Both of the babies were healthy. They were all over the moon about it. The look on Robert's face said it all, then Robert called to Annabelle's Father and he came running up the stairs and into the bedroom. He could not believe his eyes when he saw the twins, he was ecstatic.

"A boy and a girl" said the Admiral "that is perfect."

After spending some time with the new babies, Robert and his Father-in-law went downstairs to let Annabelle rest and gather her strength. They retired to the lounge to have a drink to wet the babies' heads.

In the morning, Annabelle was almost back to full strength. She was laying in bed until she had completely recovered. Robert went up to see her and sat on the bed next to her, then he put his hand in his pocket, pulled the brooch out and placed it in Annabelle's palm.

"It's beautiful" she said, with a sparkle in her eyes "where did you get it from? It must have cost a fortune."

"There's a lot more where that came from" said Robert, then he told her all about the treasure and added "our children are going to want for nothing."

They both decided to name their babies after Robert's Father, Edward, and Annabelle's Mother, Christine.

The next morning, Robert received a message from the Admiralty. He had to see Admiral Calderdale in his office, it sounded important so he went immediately.

"Good Morning Robert." Said the Admiral, sounding cheerful.

"You wanted to see me?" Asked Robert, hesitantly.

"Yes, relax; it is good news" replied the Admiral "I recommended you to be promoted to Admiral and it has been accepted. That is, if you want it. You are to be given your own fleet."

"I would be honoured" said Robert, in amazement "but can I keep my own crew?"

"I can't see why not." Said the Admiral.

Robert could not wait to tell Annabelle, who was pleased for him, although a little bit sad that she will probably see even less of him.

So everything is as it should be. Robert is now Admiral Van Helsing. They have found the treasure of the Conquistadors, which they are aloud to keep and they have rid the world of a great evil.

Or have they.

An eerie mist forms over the site of the sunken Ghost ship, the Black Orchid, screams are heard far across the Ocean. ARGHHH.

The End